CHAPTER 1

*A*bigail Clayton stood behind her desk, the phone clutched in her hand. She couldn't believe what she was hearing. "Elaine Benson? Are you sure?"

"Yes, ma'am. She passed away last Thursday," the man from the attorney's office said. She hadn't caught his name.

"How?"

"They believe she had a heart attack while working in her garden."

"She loved that garden," Abigail said softly.

"Pardon?"

"Oh, nothing. When is the funeral?"

"It's on Saturday, but I'm also calling to tell you that you will need to be at the reading of the will Friday morning."

"The will? Why?"

"Ms. Benson left you something."

Abigail's mind raced with memories that she thought she'd long since forgotten. Her father's funeral. Multiple foster homes. Finally landing at Elaine's and enjoying a couple of wonderful years before being adopted by the Clayton family in Tennessee. Even with her new family, nothing had ever compared to living with Mama Elaine, as she called her.

"Okay, what time?"

"Nine o'clock. I'll text you the address."

"Thanks."

She pressed the button to end the call and stood there, silently staring out over the Nashville skyline. Her office, on the tenth floor of the building, overlooked a line of popular bars and restaurants. Watching people had always been one of

BENEATH THE WILLOW TREE

RACHEL HANNA

her favorite pastimes. It soothed her in a weird way.

She walked closer to the window and closed her eyes, taking a deep breath. Mama Elaine was gone. It wasn't too surprising, considering she was in her eighties. The sting of regret and guilt washed over her as she thought about the last time they'd spoken. Had it really been two years ago already? How did time get away from her like that?

Abigail had adored Elaine, but life had gotten busy in recent years with a marriage, infertility, and eventual divorce. She supposed a part of her hadn't wanted to admit to Mama Elaine that she'd failed at marriage and having a baby, the two main things she'd set out to do in her life.

After losing her own father at ten years old, Abigail had ended up in foster care. Her mother had never been a part of her life, choosing to leave for another man when she was just eighteen months old. Her father had been a good man, but his drinking finally ripped him from this life when Abigail was just entering fifth grade.

After bouncing around in foster care for almost two years, she was finally placed with Elaine in Seagrove, South Carolina. At first, she'd been hesitant to bond with yet another new person, but Abigail had craved love and connection more than anything, and Elaine had that in spades.

Her two years with Elaine Benson were some of the best of her life. She'd loved her father, but his addiction had kept her from having a close relationship with him. Having never had a mother, Elaine filled that role, and Abigail had prayed she could stay there forever. As it turned out, fate had other plans. One day, she came home from school to find her social worker there, ready to collect her and take her to Tennessee.

Although she was happy to get adopted, and away from her horrible foster sister, she'd wished Elaine could be her mother. She just had that motherly demeanor that Abigail had longed for her whole life.

The Claytons were nice enough people. Her adoptive mother, Olivia, was a painter and very artsy. She was constantly redecorating their farmhouse in the mountains of Tennessee. Her adoptive father, Bruce, worked most of the time. He was a busy dentist, and his office was almost an hour from home. Abigail had always felt he was cheating on Olivia, but they stayed together anyway, probably for her sake.

"Becky?" Abigail said, poking her head out of her office. Becky had been working as her assistant at her public relations office for almost two years now, and she didn't know what she'd do without her.

"Yes?"

"I need a rental car for Thursday."

"Where are you going?" Becky asked, walking around the corner.

"Seagrove, South Carolina."

Celeste Greenway was angry. That was not unusual. Anger was one of her top three typical states of being, it seemed. It ranked right under annoyed and frustrated.

"Jim, seriously? Who thought this was okay?"

He hung his head. "I'm sorry, Celeste. I have a couple of new guys…"

"Don't pass the buck. You're the supervisor on this job. It all ends with you."

This morning, Celeste was irritated as she walked through one of the new houses in the subdivision she was developing. Somehow, a worker had managed to put a phone jack inside of a kitchen cabinet.

"I'll get it fixed."

"You know I don't like delays, Jim."

"No delays, I promise."

She stared at him for a moment longer before he hung his head and made a beeline out of there. At almost six feet tall, Celeste towered over most of the men she managed, and most of them didn't dare cross her.

As much as she sometimes wished she

was petite and sweet, God just didn't make her that way. She'd been a little rough around the edges her whole life, but what did people expect? Left at a fire station at three years old, her feelings of abandonment were deep. Trust wasn't something she gave out to just anyone, and earning it from her was almost impossible.

Her phone vibrated in her pocket, so she pressed the button on her wireless ear bud. "Hello?"

"Is this Celeste Greenway?"

"Who's asking?"

"This is Edward Dammeron, attorney at law."

"Oh, good Lord. Who's suing me now?"

He cleared his throat. "I'm Elaine Benson's attorney."

"Why is that old bat suing me?"

"No one is suing you. Elaine has… passed."

Celeste's breath caught in her throat. It wasn't often that she was surprised, but for some reason, that shocked her. Elaine

Benson was supposed to live forever. She was just that kind of force of nature. Of course, Celeste hadn't liked her. Not one bit. And she hadn't thought about her in decades.

"Are you there?"

"Yeah. Why are you calling me about this?" She popped the top on a soda can and took a long sip, desperate for a caffeine boost.

"Her funeral is this Saturday, and the will is being read Friday morning at nine."

"So?"

"Well, you're named in the will."

"What?" She almost choked on her drink.

"Ms. Benson left something to you."

"What did she leave me?" She imagined it to be an old shoe or partially chewed gum, but definitely nothing of value.

"I'm sorry, but I can't divulge anything outside of the official reading of the will."

Celeste groaned. "Do you realize I live in Texas now?"

"I do. That's why I wanted to give you

plenty of notice so you can get a plane ticket."

Her mind raced. She had an entire neighborhood under construction, and she didn't trust anyone to manage it while she was gone. However, if there was one thing Celeste couldn't stand, it was not knowing a secret. She needed to know what this woman left to her.

"Fine. I'll be there. Text me the address."

As she ended the call, she sat down on the brick fireplace hearth and stared off into space. Elaine Benson. One of her many, many foster mothers. At least Elaine hadn't been abusive like some others had been.

Celeste remembered how shocked her social worker was that she never got adopted after being abandoned at three years old. People kept coming to meet her and then deciding to go a "different direction".

"She's a little too tomboyish."

"She's so angry all the time."

"Why doesn't she smile more?"

"She won't play with dolls. She plays with trucks."

The complaints were endless. It wore on her after hearing it for so many years. To be abandoned at three years old and *never* get adopted was disheartening. But it also made her stronger than anyone she knew. Nothing pierced her thick armor.

After aging out of the foster care system, she eventually took a job framing houses with a friend's father. Year after year, she honed her craft and learned more than she could've ever imagined. Now, after almost twenty years of working in construction, she had to admit she was exhausted.

Although she loved building things, she longed for a quieter life. Being in charge was something she was good at, but didn't necessarily love. Sometimes, she just wanted to be still. Peaceful. That never happened.

Maybe this trip down memory lane would give her some kind of closure, or maybe it would open old wounds.

* * *

DIXIE TOOK a sip of her coffee. "I just can't believe it."

"How long had you known Elaine?" Julie asked, reaching across and squeezing her hand.

"Almost fifty years," she said, her eyes welling with tears. "She was older than me, but we were dear friends. In fact, we ran the gardening club together for almost ten years before we passed the baton to the younger folks a few years back."

"I'm so sorry, Dixie. Losing someone you love is so hard."

"Don't I know it. Losing Johnny just about killed me."

"Is there anything I can do?"

Dixie smiled sadly. "Do you mind if I head home and take a nice hot bath? I think I need to have a good cry in private."

"Of course. How about I bring you a casserole later? Lucy has tons of them in the freezer for just this sort of occasion."

"Oh, that's alright, dear. I'm not very hungry."

"Is Harry home?"

"No. He's visiting his daughter this week."

"Do you want me to come by after work?"

Dixie stood up. "I think I just want to be alone, if that's okay? I need a little quiet time to grieve."

"Okay, but if you need anything, you know how to reach me," Julie said, hugging her. Dixie picked up her purse and walked out as Julie watched her and worried. She was truly like a second mother to her.

As Julie unpacked a box of romance novels, Janine walked into the shop. "Hey, sis. What's wrong with Dixie? She looked so sad when I passed her on the sidewalk just now."

Julie waved for her to sit down and handed her a cup of coffee. This was their regular routine in the mornings before Janine's first yoga class of the day. One cup of coffee with extra cream and sugar, and a banana nut muffin.

"She just lost a friend. Her name was Elaine Benson."

"Oh wow. Ms. Benson, who owned the house with that enormous willow tree?"

Julie sat down across from her and took a sip from her second cup of coffee. "You knew her?"

"Not well, but we met a couple of times. She did my senior yoga class, but I haven't seen her in months. I guess I should've checked in on her."

"Dixie is pretty torn up about it. They'd been friends for fifty years."

"Fifty years? Wow. That's amazing."

"Yeah. I don't have a friend like that," Julie said, feeling a little sadness. Since leaving Atlanta, she'd thought a lot about friendship. The women she'd hung around with back in those days had been so shallow, yet they were all she'd had at the time.

"You have me and Dixie!"

"I had a wonderful childhood friend, but we didn't stay in touch. Maybe I should've tried harder."

"Do you mean Carol?" Janine asked, scrunching her nose.

"What was wrong with Carol?"

"She was horrible! I've never met a kid who was meaner than her."

Julie chuckled. "Okay, maybe she was, but if I'd have stayed friends with her, we'd be coming up on forty years of friendship."

Janine rolled her eyes. "She's probably in jail by now. Maybe you can go on visitation day."

"You're terrible!"

As Abigail pulled her car into the parking space in front of Edward Dammeron's office, she felt so much nostalgia it was hard to breathe. She hadn't been to Seagrove in years. The memories she had were surprisingly good. Elaine had been a wonderful foster mother, and they did a lot of things together, like going to get ice cream and taking walks around the town square.

She got out of her car and took in a deep breath of the salty sea air that permeated the downtown area. It made her immediately happy to smell it. She loved living in Tennessee, but the ocean had always called to her and made her feel at home in a way she couldn't put into words.

"Can I help you with anything, hon?" She turned toward the office building and saw a younger woman dressed in a business suit smiling at her.

"Oh, I was just taking a walk down memory lane."

"Pardon?"

"Nothing. Do you happen to know which suite is Edward Dammeron's office?"

She smiled. "I'm his assistant, Diane. He's in suite two. I was just running to get some coffee. Would you like any?"

"No, thank you."

She watched Diane walk down the sidewalk before turning to go into the building. Her stomach gurgled and churned. She hated surprises and always had. It was far easier to know all the details well in advance so she could relax. Anticipatory anxiety was her constant enemy.

Abigail pulled the handle of the large oak door. The building was older and historic, with high ceilings and original hardwood floors. There was a bit of a musty smell, much like that of an old library. Places like this had style, unlike all the newer construction she'd seen around Nashville. She hated those kinds of neighborhoods where every house looked the same, and each lot was the size of a postage stamp. What they did to the trees and area wildlife made her sick to her stomach.

Since Diane was gone to get coffee, there was no one at the front desk, so she took a seat in one of the brown leather chairs. The waiting area was small, and there was one table with some old southern architecture magazines and a weathered copy of People magazine. Nondescript was a great way to describe the office. She didn't have to wait long, as it turned out.

"Are you here for the reading of Elaine Benson's will?" A man she assumed to be Mr. Dammeron asked as he popped his head around the doorway.

"Yes. I'm Abigail Clayton."

"Great. Come on back!"

She followed him down a short hallway into an office. It was a cluttered mess, with papers and files all over his giant mahogany desk and a wall of books on the shelves behind him. Edward Dammeron was a bit of a mess himself with his loosened neck tie and unwieldy hairstyle.

"Please, have a seat. The other party will join us soon, I hope."

Other party? Abigail hadn't thought about there being "other parties". Of course, it would only make sense that Elaine would leave things to multiple people and not just her, especially since she'd only been her foster daughter for two years. It wasn't like she was the center of Elaine's world or anything.

Mr. Dammeron walked out of the room

and Abigail looked out the window to her left. His office had a view of the marsh, and she realized how much she missed that. There was just something about the sights and smells of the lowcountry. A part of her had never left, even though she hadn't been back in decades.

So many times, she'd planned to go visit Elaine, but life always got in the way. First, she met Danny in college and they'd gotten married a few months after graduation. He was supposed to be her lifelong partner, but it hadn't turned out that way. Infertility, money fights and infidelity had plagued their marriage, and now she found herself divorced and childless at thirty-eight years old. It wasn't exactly the plan she had laid out for herself so many years ago.

After her divorce, she threw herself further into her public relations business, working long hours to avoid her empty condo. Danny was the life of every party, totally the opposite of her reserved personality.

Once he wasn't living there anymore, the place felt hollow and sterile.

"Sorry for the delay. We called the other party, and they said they're parking now. We'll get started any minute," Mr. Dammeron said, poking his head around the corner. Abigail nodded and smiled slightly.

"No problem." She really didn't have anywhere to go, anyway. She'd taken a full week off, intent on spending some time in nearby Charleston and maybe even going to the beach. She hadn't taken a vacation in years. The last one was with Danny when they went to Tampa, Florida, for one of his business conventions. She'd spent most of the time in the room researching infertility doctors, not knowing Danny was spending most of his time in a room one floor below theirs with some woman named Sophie who was now his pregnant wife. Life wasn't always fair.

Mr. Dammeron scurried back into the room and sat behind his desk. "The other party is here, but had to use the restroom."

"Okay," she said, not wanting any more details.

"How was your drive into Seagrove?" he asked, obviously trying to make small talk.

"Very nice. I forgot how tall that bridge is in Charleston, though. Gave me some anxiety." She hated heights.

"Ah, yes. It can be a little daunting to some folks." He looked to his left, toward the door to the office. "Oh good. Here she comes."

The door opened, and one of the tallest women she'd ever seen walked through. She was wearing a stained pair of jeans, work boots and a black t-shirt. Her brown hair was pulled into a tight ponytail. Abigail scanned up to her face and felt like she was about to swallow her tongue.

"Ms. Clayton, do you know Ms. Greenway?"

CHAPTER 2

*C*eleste stared at the woman sitting in the chair in front of her. Almost twenty-four years had passed since she'd seen that face, but she would've known it anywhere. Abigail.

"Abigail Ellison?"

"It's actually Clayton now. My adopted name."

The word "adopted" stung a little. Abigail, the perfect little foster kid, was adopted a couple of years after arriving at Elaine's. One day, Celeste came home from riding her skateboard to find Abigail gone. Adopted. Lucky.

The two had been forced to share a room because Elaine had other foster kids and she was renovating some of the other rooms in the large Victorian house. Of course, Celeste always believed that Elaine had thrown them together simply to drive Celeste nuts.

She and Abigail were nothing alike, and judging by the prim and proper business suit she was currently wearing, it looked like not much had changed. The nerdy little girl had turned into a nerdy adult woman. Same nerd, different outfit.

"Please, have a seat and we'll get started," Mr. Dammeron said, pointing to the chair beside Abigail. Celeste pulled the back of the chair toward her and away from Abigail, and sat down. Mr. Dammeron cleared his throat, obviously aware of the tension in the room. "Thank you both for coming today. I'm sure the news of Elaine Benson's loss hit you terribly." He looked at each of them.

"Well, she was pretty old, so…" Celeste said, crossing her arms.

Abigail stared at her. "Elaine was a wonderful woman, and I was so sad to hear she died. I hadn't spoken to her in almost two years, and I feel so guilty about that."

Celeste rolled her eyes. Abigail - always saying the right thing. Always looking for the attention. Yuck.

"I'm sure she understood," Mr. Dammeron said. "After all, you two are her only heirs."

Celeste felt like she was going to choke. "What? Just the two of us? But, she had dozens of foster kids over the years. And certainly some family?"

"No, Elaine had no family. As you know, she never had biological kids, never adopted. Her sister died many years ago, and she never had kids either."

"What about other foster kids, then?" Abigail asked.

"Nope. She left specific instructions that

you two were her only heirs. She left everything to you with certain conditions."

"*Everything?*" Celeste reiterated.

"Yes, everything."

"I'm in absolute shock. Why would she do
that?" Abigail asked.

"She left a letter to be read at the reading
of her will. Maybe that will shed some light. I
wasn't supposed to open it until now, but
here goes," he said, using a gold metal letter
opener to slice the envelope. *"Dear Abigail
and Celeste, I know my death may have come as
a shock to you..."*

Celeste almost chuckled. The woman was
in her eighties. Death wasn't exactly shocking, especially since Celeste hadn't talked to
her in decades. As far as she knew, Elaine
had been dead since the day after she left the
woman's house.

*"You might wonder why I have left all of my
earthly possessions to the two of you."*

The thought did cross my mind, Celeste
thought to herself.

"Over all of my years as a foster mother, two

girls stood out to me the most. The two of you were such polar opposites, and I never forgot you. When it came time to decide what to do with my estate, there was no question. You see, you two girls needed me more than any other children who came to stay with me."

Wait, what? Celeste couldn't believe her ears. They needed her? She needed no one!

"Abigail, you were such a fragile child, always needing comfort and love. I adored spending time with you because it made me feel like a mother. I'd always wanted to be a mother, but it was never in the cards for me. Sure, I could've adopted, but if I had done so, then I wouldn't have had the space to take in so many foster children. I felt God wanted me to be the mother of many children rather than just one or two."

How much longer was this letter? Celeste was getting hungry and wanted a bucket of fried chicken from that southern restaurant she passed on the way into town.

"And Celeste. Oh, my dear, you were the hardest kid I ever had. You were contrary about everything. There was never a moment that you

looked peaceful. There was never a moment where I felt I could hug you without fear of getting bitten or scratched. Your wall was thicker and taller than anything the ancient Egyptians could've even dreamed up!"

"Lovely," Celeste muttered under her breath.

"Under all of that gruff exterior, you were just aching for love. Attention. Someone you could count on. As hard as I tried, I never quite got there with you. When social services moved you to that group home, I cried for days with worry."

What? She cried over her? Celeste wasn't buying it. These were obviously the musings of an old woman struggling with memory loss or trying to get into heaven.

"What I'm trying to say is that I loved you girls, but you both needed different things. I know you didn't get along well..."

"That's an understatement," Celeste said quietly.

"But I remember one day when I looked out the front window and saw the two of you sitting

beneath the willow tree. You were talking and laughing like friends."

"She obviously had memory issues," Celeste said, looking at Abigail, who shushed her.

"I knew there was hope for you two to become sisters. And that is why I have decided to go this route. I am leaving the house, all of its contents, and my car to you girls. Each of you owns half of everything. But there is one caveat."

"Of course there is," Celeste said with a groan.

"You must live in the house together for three months. Work together to use the house for something good, like I did. After three months, you will explain what you've done to three of my best friends who will decide if you really gave it your best shot. Did you create something beautiful that will help the world? If not, the house will be sold, and the money donated to charity. If you do something great together, you can keep the house, or you can walk away. Sell the place, split the profits, whatever you need to do. I just want to know that you girls got to know each

other in a real way and did something good together."

Celeste stood up quickly. "This is the most idiotic thing I've ever heard! I came all the way from Texas for this?" She turned to walk toward the door.

"Ms. Greenway, please just give me a few more minutes of your time."

She sighed and crossed her arms, unwilling to sit back down. "You have five minutes." Celeste looked over at Abigail, who still sat there all prim and proper, seemingly unaffected by the latest news. "What do you have to say about all of this?"

Abigail shrugged her shoulders. "I mean, it's an interesting offer. I love that old house."

Celeste's mouth dropped open. "We don't like each other. Can you imagine living together again for three entire months? And working together on some mystery project before being judged by three old biddies? It sounds like the definition of hell on earth to me."

Abigail rolled her eyes. "I see you still have the same personality."

"Ladies, please. Let's not make this personal," Mr. Dammeron said, trying to rein the conversation in and back to the topic at hand.

"Can I just say no and get back on the road?" Celeste asked.

"If you say no, the whole deal is off. The house will be sold and the profits will be donated to a cat charity."

Celeste stared at him. "A *cat charity*? You can't be serious? I thought she'd donate to foster kids or something?"

Mr. Dammeron smiled slightly. "Elaine hated cats. She was highly allergic, in fact."

"Then why donate to a charity for cats? That house must be worth at least half a million dollars, if not more."

"I looked it up a couple of years ago when she asked me to help her with some financial stuff. Even back then, it was worth close to a million dollars," Abigail said.

"I suppose she wanted you to know just

how serious she was about this. Maybe she figured neither of you would be okay letting all that money go to cats. Can I finish the letter?"

Celeste slowly sat back down, keeping her arms crossed. "Go ahead."

"I know Celeste will be angry about this, and Abigail will probably agree to try it. I'm not doing this as a punitive thing, and I want you to know that. You girls were family for a time, and having family is so important. This is my chance to give you exactly what you've always needed - each other. I love you both. Do good!"

There was a silence that hung over the room as Mr. Dammeron folded the letter and slipped it back into the envelope before placing it in the folder. He put his hands on the folder and looked at each of them. "Well?"

"When do we have to decide?" Abigail asked.

"I suppose by tomorrow would be best."

"Maybe we can go back to our hotels and think about it?" Abigail said.

"Actually, Elaine left the keys to the house for you. You're welcome to stay there. Maybe it will help you make up your minds?"

Celeste stared straight ahead. She wanted to say no and walk out the door. That fried chicken was calling her name. But this was a million dollar house, and people didn't just walk around handing out checks for half a million dollars. She could use her share of the money to change her entire life. As much as she hated the idea, she figured she should at least consider it. After all, three months wasn't *that* long.

"Yes, why don't we stay at the house? Chat about it?"

Abigail looked at her, surprise written all over her face. "Really?"

"Absolutely. First, though, I'm going to pick up some fried chicken."

ABIGAIL STOOD under the big willow tree and looked up into its thick green branches. "Do you remember us sitting here and laughing together?"

Celeste popped the last bite of a chicken leg into her mouth before dropping the bone into the empty paper bucket with a thud. "Nope. I don't remember the two of us ever laughing unless it was me making fun of you."

Memories flooded Abigail's mind as she stared at the old house, which was still as beautiful as ever. "I have so many wonderful memories of this place."

"Glad one of us does." Celeste was sitting on the ground, her back leaned against the tree. She was just as rough around the edges as ever. The thought of living with her again was about as appealing as kissing a shark on the lips.

"Surely you have fond memories of Mama Elaine."

"Mama Elaine? Seriously? You always were a kiss-up, but I thought you might've grown out of it by now." She stood up and stared at the house, her hands on her hips.

"I loved her."

"Oh yeah? When was the last time you came to see her, Abby?"

Abigail swallowed hard. "It's been a long time, but I called her a couple of times a year. I mean, I didn't the last two years because life just got in the way…"

"Life got in the way of you making a phone call?"

"Look, I had some stuff happening in my personal life and I just didn't feel like sharing it with her. I already feel guilty enough." She started walking toward the front porch. Celeste followed.

"Guilt is a useless emotion, Abs."

Abigail turned around. "Don't call me Abs. I can handle Abby, but I prefer Abigail."

Celeste put up her hands. "Fine. Don't freak out." She walked past Abigail and trotted up the front steps. "Where's the key?"

Abigail pulled it from her pocket and handed it to Celeste. "When was the last time you talked to Elaine?"

"The day I left this place and went to the group home."

"What? You seriously never talked to her again?"

"Yep," Celeste said, not looking up as she turned the lock and opened the door.

As the door swung open, Abigail was immediately overcome with memories. The smell of Elaine's perfume hung in the air like a welcoming hug. They stepped inside, and she was struck by the way the house looked exactly the same as it did when she was a kid. She remembered those first moments walking through that same doorway, wondering what the rest of her life would look like. Would she live with foster parents until she was eighteen, or would someone else want her to be their daughter? Abigail could still feel the fear of her ten-year-old self. The uncertainty. The grief.

"Wow. This place looks exactly the same."

Celeste scrunched her nose. "Yeah, and it smells like that awful perfume Elaine wore. It was so musky."

"I liked it," Abigail said, walking past her and into the foyer.

"Maybe she left a bottle upstairs. I think they stopped making it in the eighties, though."

Ignoring Celeste's constant snide comments, Abigail slowly walked into the living room. When she was a kid, Elaine spent a lot of time in there reading and crocheting. She was a master at crocheting, always making hats and gloves that she would send to foster parents in colder parts of the country.

She walked around the room, running her fingers across finished blankets laying across the back of the sofa. Memories zipped through her brain like little movies. They were going so fast, she couldn't catch them all as they slipped through her fingers.

"I can feel her here."

Celeste stared at her. "Okay…"

Abigail had had enough. "Why did you even come to Seagrove if you were going to act like a jerk?"

"Excuse me?"

"You've been nothing but rude since you got here. Why do you have such a chip on your shoulder? Elaine was an angel. Do you know how many kids she took care of in her life? What have you done?"

Abigail's heart raced. She hated confrontation with a passion.

"What have I done? Well, I've raised myself from the age of three while being bounced around from one set of crappy foster parents to another. I've paid my way, gone from sleeping in my ratty old truck to actually owning a house. I learned a trade and have been well paid for two decades in my industry. What have you done?"

"I've been nice to people."

Celeste laughed and rolled her eyes. "Wow. Impressive."

"You might want to try it sometime."

"Being nice is overrated. Plus, I have no desire to let people walk all over me." She leaned against the bannister.

"People don't walk all over me."

"No? Where's your husband, by the way?"

Abigail's blood felt like it was literally boiling in her veins. "How do you know about my husband?"

"I guess I'm smarter than you think I am. One look at your Facebook page on the way through the drive-thru line at the chicken place told me all I needed to know."

"Look, I'm not falling for this," she said, walking past her and sitting down in Elaine's favorite armchair. It still looked new because she'd kept it covered all those years.

"Falling for what?" Celeste sat down on the sofa across from her and leaned back, her arms crossed against her chest.

"When we were kids, you did this all the time. You would antagonize me until I was either crying or escaping to get away from you. We're adults now, and you don't intimidate me, Celeste." Even as Abigail said it, she knew she was lying. Her stomach felt like a knot of angry snakes.

"Yeah, yeah, yeah. Look, we came here to talk about this whole house situation. Why don't we just do that?"

"Fine. Let's do it."

* * *

JULIE LEANED back against the chair, a cup of coffee in her hands. She looked out over the ocean and smiled. There was just nothing better than sitting on the deck and looking over the water at the end of a long day at work. The bookstore wasn't usually a stressful place to work, but a huge shipment had come in that day. Every muscle in her body was sore.

As if on cue, Dawson walked up behind her and squeezed her aching shoulders. "How did you know I needed that?" she asked, leaning her head back and smiling at him.

Dawson chuckled. "Because you always need that after a big shipment." He walked around the other chair and sat down next to her.

"So, how was your day?"

"Good. I took Dylan to get his school supplies, and I heard from an old friend."

"Oh yeah? Who?"

"His name is Ben Callaway. We went to middle school together before his family moved away right before our freshman year in high school."

"Why did they move away from here?" she asked. Julie was always dumbfounded when she saw someone put a for sale sign in their yard. Who would ever leave Seagrove?

"His dad got a job out west. I think he was an engineer or something."

"What made him contact you?"

"We've kept in touch on social media for the last few years. He's newly divorced and looking for a change, so he's coming back to Seagrove."

"Well, I can say for sure that Seagrove is a great place to start over. When's the last time he was here?"

Dawson smiled. "Eighth grade."

"I'm sure a lot has changed since then," she said, laughing.

"Not nearly as much as you'd think."

"When does he arrive?"

"Next week. He tried to tell me he rented a room at an extended stay motel until he can find an apartment."

"And I'm sure you invited him to stay at the inn?" She knew her husband very well, and he was never going to let an old friend stay at some ratty motel when he had a perfectly good inn.

"Of course."

She reached over and squeezed his hand. "You're the sweetest man I know."

Dawson chuckled. "Listen, I don't mind when you say stuff like that to me, but please don't say it in front of Ben. He might just take my man card away."

CHAPTER 3

*C*eleste stirred the mashed potatoes one last time and then took a bite to make sure they were creamy enough for her liking. There was nothing worse than lumpy mashed potatoes. Her secret to the perfect mashed potatoes was to sauté onions and garlic in a pan and then put them in a blender with milk or cream. She used that mixture instead of plain milk and it was always a hit with anyone who ate them.

Of course, she wasn't exactly hosting a lot of dinner parties. She lived in a small three-bedroom house alone, and she hadn't developed a close circle of friends in Texas. Her years of moving around hadn't helped her develop bonds with people, but it was more her unwillingness to open herself up to anyone. Life had proven that was a losing and dangerous game for her to play.

The only one she could count on was herself.

"What are you doing?" Abigail asked as she walked into the kitchen.

"Well, we have to eat, don't we?"

The two of them had avoided each other for most of the day, even though they were supposed to be discussing the giant elephant in the room. Celeste had no idea what she wanted to do about Elaine's house. The thought of staying in Seagrove for months and living with Abigail under the same roof again made her want to vomit. She enjoyed living alone.

"I guess I didn't know you cooked," she said, sitting down at the breakfast bar. It looked like Elaine had gotten the kitchen renovated in the last few years because now it had the breakfast bar, a built-in desk and granite countertops.

Celeste looked at her. "Well, as a kid, I didn't cook. As a single adult woman with hands, I learned to cook a long time ago." Abigail rolled her eyes.

"A simple 'yes, I know how to cook' would've sufficed."

"Yes, I know how to cook."

"I can pick something up from that cafe down the street, so don't worry about me."

Celeste stared at her. "First of all, I wasn't worried about you. Second, I cooked a lot of food, so you'll eat it and like it, okay?"

"Why are you so abrasive and bossy?"

"Why are you so boring and dull?"

Abigail pursed her lips. "Thanks for cooking," she said through gritted teeth. "What did you make?"

"Country-fried steak, mashed potatoes, green beans."

"Wow. I could've helped if you'd asked. I was outside in Elaine's garden. I picked some zucchini." She held up two large zucchini squash.

"I don't eat healthy food."

"You're eating green beans."

"From a can with a big dollop of butter. I'd hardly call that healthy."

Celeste finished working at the stove and then retrieved two dinner plates from the cabinet. She slid one across the counter toward Abigail.

"I don't serve."

"I didn't expect you to."

The level of tension when they were near each other was more than palpable. It hung in the air like a thick fog, and Celeste knew she was the main contributor to it. She could hold her tongue. She could just play nice. But something inside of her wouldn't allow that. Abigail's mere presence made her want to lash out and say ugly things.

She made her plate and sat at the kitchen table, assuming that Abigail would make her way back to the breakfast bar. Instead, she made a plate and sat across from Celeste.

"You'd have more room at the bar."

"Celeste, we need to talk about all of this. It's almost bedtime, and Elaine's service is in the morning."

"The sun's barely setting, and you're talking about bedtime? What are you? A pioneer woman?"

She could see Abigail's jaw clench a bit, but the woman wouldn't lose her cool. She'd always been that way. A "go along" kind of person. Easygoing. The kind everyone likes because she blends in like a chameleon. The type of woman who has no opinion unless someone tells her to have one. If she were a color, it would be beige.

"I like to get my rest. It's good for your brain. Did you know your brain basically cleans itself between ten pm and two am?"

Celeste stared at her and went back to eating her food. "I'm not going to the service, anyway."

"What?"

"I don't make a habit of going to funerals for people I didn't like and who didn't like me."

"Celeste, come on. She left the house to us. She obviously loved you."

"That's not how I remember it at all. Elaine Benson liked you, but she definitely didn't like me."

Abigail took a bite of potatoes. "Well, you were a bit difficult, to be fair. You were constantly sneaking out, smoking behind the church, stealing from the candy store…"

"Did you keep a log of my misdeeds? Anyway, I was a kid. An abandoned kid. What did you expect?"

"So was I," Abigail said quietly. Celeste slammed her fork onto the table.

"No! I won't let you get away with saying that. You were raised by your father until you were like ten years old. I got dropped off at a fire station when I was three, like some kind of useless trash. Not the same!"

"Celeste…"

"Do you know what it's like to have

someone keep you for three years and still let you go? It wasn't like I was a baby. I was someone's *child*, but I wasn't good enough to keep. I wasn't loved enough for my own mother to keep me. You were loved by your father and then loved by Elaine. So don't you ever say we had the same experience because we didn't." She looked back down at her plate and stared at it, wishing she had kept her mouth shut. Vulnerability wasn't her strong suit. Her face burned, and her eyes welled with tears of frustration, but she willed the fluid right back into her tear ducts.

Abigail's eyes widened. She paused for a moment before speaking. "You're right."

"What?"

"You're right. I never really thought about how we were different."

For once, Celeste didn't know what to say. "Well, we were."

Dinner was quiet after that, with Celeste's stomach staying in knots the whole time. She hated how this place made her feel.

Memories kept washing over her, but she pushed them away. Even good memories, the few she had, made her want to scream. She'd long ago wiped this place from her memory, much like the other homes she'd stayed in. Why had Elaine chosen her, of all people, to get half of this house? It made no sense.

"Can we talk about the house?" Abigail finally asked.

"Fine. Let's get it over with. I can't stay here."

"Why?"

"For one thing, I'm the contractor in charge of the development of a neighborhood in Texas. I can't do that job from here."

"I see."

"I have a life there. A house."

"Could you rent it out?"

"Probably, but I can't rent out my job. Besides, don't you have a life back where you live?"

"In Nashville? I have a condo and a job in public relations."

"Sounds super exciting," Celeste said dryly.

"Actually, it's a great job. It's just not what I want to do for the rest of my life."

"What do you want to do?"

She shrugged her shoulders. "Be a wife and mom."

"Gag."

"Can you just try to be nice for five minutes? You know, like a human?" Abigail said, her nostrils flaring.

"Fine," she said, taking a bite of green beans. "So you want to move into the house?"

"Maybe. It sounds like a fun adventure."

Celeste tried to keep from rolling her eyes but wasn't successful. "Well, I can't."

"You should at least come to the service."

"I'm not a faker. I can't stand there and pretend I'll miss a woman I hadn't even seen in decades."

"Maybe the closure would be good for you."

Celeste chuckled. "Closure? Has someone been in therapy?"

"Yes, I actually have. It helps."

"I'll take your word for it."

Abigail picked up her plate and rinsed it in the sink. "You've never been to therapy?"

"Nope," she said before taking a last sip of her tea. "And I don't plan to go. I don't need some head shrinker to tell me about my life."

"Well, I'll give you a friendly piece of advice."

"Oh, please do."

"When you've had trauma in your life, you have to deal with it before it deals with you."

"Did you read that on a bumper sticker or something?"

Abigail smiled sadly. "Celeste, I know you're in pain, and until you deal with it, you'll never get what you want in life."

Celeste walked over and put her plate in the sink. "I already have what I want, and it's in Texas." She was lying, of course. She didn't have what she wanted, and she didn't even know what that was.

* * *

"So, when are we dress shopping?" Julie asked her sister as they sat on the deck at the inn. It was one of their favorite things to do. They would sit and talk after dinner, catching up on the week's events.

"I don't know. It seems a little weird to buy a proper wedding dress at my age."

Julie stared at her. "You're in your forties, Janine. And this is your first wedding."

Janine laughed. "First? Let's hope it's my *only* wedding, sis."

"Sorry. That came out wrong."

"William and I can't decide what kind of wedding we want. On the one hand, something small and intimate on the beach is calling to me. On the other hand, I've waited my whole life for this, so it feels like I should go all 'royal wedding' or something."

"I don't think a royal wedding is really you," Julie said, squeezing her hand.

"No? You don't think a ten-foot train and renting a cathedral is the way to go?"

Julie laughed. "Probably not."

"I just want it to be a memorable day."

"When you marry the man of your dreams, it's a day you'll never forget, no matter what the wedding ceremony looks like. Trust me. The marriage is so much more important than a ceremony."

"I know you're right," she said, nodding as she looked at Julie.

She really wanted to have a special day with William, but every day was special with him, anyway. Maybe Julie was right, and she was putting too much pressure on making it perfect. Did all brides feel this way?

"There's my fiancee," William said from behind as he walked over and squeezed her shoulders. He and Dawson had gone over to the barn after dinner so Dawson could show him a new table he was making for the bookstore.

Dixie and Julie had decided to remodel the cafe area to make more seating and an area for musical entertainment. They were planning to stay open later on weekends and allow local music artists to play for customers. It would bring in more sales of coffee and books, or at least that was the hope.

"And there's my hot wife," Dawson said, leaning over and kissing the top of Julie's head. Janine loved to watch their relationship. Seeing Julie thrive after what her ex-husband had put her through made Janine so happy. She hoped her own marriage would be as strong, and she believed it would.

William and Dawson weren't the same. William was more reserved and less open about his feelings in front of others. Dawson was that much desired swoon worthy romance character that all women seemed to want. He was like a Prince Charming come to life. Since their engagement, she had noticed William being more open in public, and it was kind of nice.

Of course, William proposed in a very public way, so she had to give him that. It was completely out of character and shocking, so she'd never forget the moment they got engaged. She wanted her wedding to be the same. Unforgettable.

Dawson sat down next to Julie, taking her hand. William did the same. They all stared out over the water for a moment. Janine would never get tired of the view. For someone who'd traveled around the world for most of her adult life, she couldn't imagine ever leaving Seagrove.

"So, have you ladies come up with anything related to the wedding?" William asked.

"It seems Janine is preparing either a royal wedding with an expensive designer dress or possibly just wearing jeans at the justice of the peace," Julie joked.

"Hey, I'm open minded!" Janine said, laughing.

"I've told her a million times that I will do

whatever she wants. I just want to be married."

"Aw, aren't you just a sweetie?" Dawson said, poking fun at William.

"Shut up."

"What about a beach wedding?" Julie suggested.

"I don't know. It's just been done to death, you know?"

Julie laughed. "Yeah, we all hate the beach."

"You know what I mean. I want something memorable."

"We could jump out of an airplane," William said, laughing.

"Oh, I like that idea! And you could have a little flower girl holding onto the train of your princess dress like her life depends on it!"

William tossed an empty water bottle at Dawson. "You'd better stop joking around, man! Weddings are serious business with the ladies."

Janine stared at him for a moment. "So, you don't care about our wedding?"

"Uh oh…" Dawson whispered to Julie.

"Of course I do. It's just not as important to me as it is to you, sweetie. Guys don't tend to care about wedding venues or cake flavors."

She crossed her arms over her chest and stared out over the water. "I guess I just assumed you'd care as much as I do about our one and only wedding day."

Janine didn't know why she was mad. Of course, guys didn't think about wedding preparations like women did. For some reason, she wanted William to be as invested as she was.

"Janine, don't be mad at me. I want to get married. You know that. I just don't care if it's a big wedding or at the courthouse. All I care about is that you are my wife at the end."

She took in a deep breath and blew it out. "I know. I think I'm just a little stressed."

He leaned over and kissed her cheek. "We'll figure it out."

* * *

ABIGAIL STOOD beside the flower-draped casket, her eyes swollen from crying. She wished she could talk to Mama Elaine one more time, tell her she was sorry for losing touch. Explain how she'd run her life off the rails and ask for advice. None of those things were possible now.

Seeing Elaine at the church, her casket open in front of the pulpit, made her feel hollow inside. For all intents and purposes, she'd always thought of her as her mother. Their bond had stood the test of time until Abigail had dropped the ball so horribly.

"Hey there," a woman said quietly from behind her. She turned around to see someone she recognized slightly, like a blurry memory buried in the back of her brain somewhere.

"Hi," Abigail said, forcing a smile.

"I'm Dixie. You probably don't remember me since you were just a little girl the last time I saw you. Abigail, right?"

She smiled. "Yes, ma'am. Sorry, I don't quite remember…"

Dixie waved her hand. "Sugar, it's no big deal. It was a long time ago. Elaine was one of my dearest friends. I used to come have coffee with her from time to time. We'd watch you kids play out in the yard or get off the school bus."

Abigail turned back to the casket. "I can't believe she's gone." She placed her hand against the cold, shiny wood. A huge oak tree hung over them, casting a shadow and providing a bit of relief from the already increasing heat of the day.

"I can't either. She was such a wonderful woman. Did so many great things for people."

"I suppose you've heard about her will?" Abigail asked, turning back toward her.

Dixie smiled. "Yes, I heard. She was quite a character. It only makes sense she'd do something like that as the ultimate act of kindness."

"I'm not sure it's going to work out. The other woman she left the house to… Celeste… well, she's not exactly on board for this adventure."

"And you would be?"

Abigail shrugged her shoulders. "I could handle a little adventure."

Dixie put her hand on Abigail's shoulder and smiled slyly. "Then you let old Dixie handle Celeste, okay?"

* * *

CELESTE PEEKED AROUND THE TREE, trying desperately to stay out of sight. Somehow, she'd managed to hide at the back of the church, a pair of dark sunglasses on her face. As soon as she'd gotten to the funeral, she'd wished she hadn't made the last-minute decision to go.

Something inside of her kept nagging at her until she finally got dressed and went.

Listening to the pastor talk about Elaine like she was some kind of saint made Celeste nauseous. The woman wasn't that nice to everyone, and she was living proof.

A part of her felt guilty for having such hard feelings against a woman who was dead now. Another part of her was mad at everyone. It was a hard way to live.

As she watched Abigail talk to some random woman near the casket, she thought about her time in Seagrove all those years ago. The town was nice enough, but it had been boring to a teenage girl who just wanted to have some fun. Sow her wild oats. Make some memories.

School had been a nightmare. Celeste had never fit in anywhere, and middle school was a prime example of that. Not only was she known as a foster kid, but she hadn't done well in her classes either. Teachers didn't like her, and she spent most of her time in detention or in the principal's office. Elaine was constantly coming to parent-teacher conferences or meetings with the principal.

Being taller than every boy in her school wasn't a picnic, either. She towered above everyone in the class pictures, including the teachers. Feeling like she was always on display, like some kind of circus freak, made her bristle more than the average kid.

Finally, Abigail walked back toward the square, talking with the woman. Celeste looked around and didn't see anyone apart from some of the funeral home staff who were on the other side of the cemetery, setting up for another burial. She slowly walked toward Elaine's gravesite, unsure of what she was even doing there.

She stood in front of the casket and looked down at the flower arrangement draping over it. It was a mixture of flowers in just about every color with a big pink bow on it. Why did we wrap up dead people's caskets like we were giving them away as presents? *"Here, God, happy Saturday! Enjoy hanging out with Elaine for eternity!"*

"Hello," she mumbled softly, looking around again before speaking. "I just want you to know I'm here because I don't want you haunting me or something."

Without warning, a red cardinal flew by and landed right on the tree above her, startling Celeste.

"Not funny," she said, shooing the bird with her hand until it flew away. Hopefully, no one saw her talking to herself and flailing her arms at a bird. They might just drive her right to the loony bin. "Listen, I don't know why you gave this house to me and Abigail, but I can't take it, okay? I have a life back in Texas, and it wasn't fair of you to assume I would come back here."

Celeste didn't know what she expected from this one-sided conversation, but if Elaine suddenly popped the top of the casket and responded, she was running for her life.

"I just want you to know that I actually do appreciate the gesture because you were kind of rotten to me back then. You made me feel like you didn't like me, and you only liked Abigail. Why did you do that?"

Out of nowhere, she could feel tears filling her eyes. She wasn't a crier. In fact, she couldn't remember the last time she'd cried. It had to be many years ago.

"Anyway, I can't do this. I just can't. I left this place behind a long time ago. And no, my life now isn't perfect, but it's mine. I control it. I'm in charge. People respect me. I can't come back here, not even for three months. You got that?" Her jaw clenched as she wiped the stray - and very unwelcome - tears away and turned toward the house.

She had to get out of this town.

CHAPTER 4

anine stood in front of the full-length mirror and stared at herself. Surely she didn't look as goofy as she felt. "I don't like these sleeves."

"Yeah, they look kind of big on you," Julie said, trying to smooth them down onto Janine's small, toned arms. Yoga did a body good.

"Let me go grab the one with the sweetheart neckline. I think I have one in your size in the back," the saleswoman said, disappearing into the stockroom.

Janine dropped the dress onto the floor

and stepped out of it. Julie picked it up and laid it over the back of the red velvet settee that was in the changing area. The dress shop, just outside of Seagrove, was the best in the area. They could go into Charleston, of course, but Janine didn't want to deal with traffic and crowds.

"Nothing seems right," she said, frustrated. Was wedding planning supposed to be this hard?

"Are you sure you don't want to try Charleston?"

"Not today. There are hundreds of dresses here. Surely I can find one."

"Maybe strapless?"

Janine laughed. "Sis, I have nothing that would hold up a strapless dress."

"I'm not saying a word."

"God blessed you in that area. Me, not so much. So, have you heard from the girls lately?"

"They did a video chat with me last night. It looks beautiful where they are now."

Meg, Christian, Colleen and Tucker had

taken off on an adventure, traveling around the country with little Vivi in tow. Dixie and Harry had been kind enough to let them borrow their motorhome to make some life-time memories. They'd been gone two weeks now, and Janine could tell Julie missed them terribly. At least she had Dylan to keep her busy.

Sometimes Janine felt envious of her sister. She had kids, a grandkid, a great husband and a wonderful business. Janine was grateful to have her yoga business, and she adored William, but she felt like something was missing. Maybe that was why she was so insistent on making her wedding perfect.

"Where are they?"

"Steamboat Springs, Colorado."

"I've seen pictures, and that is a gorgeous part of the country. When do Meg and Christian have to be back at work at the college?"

"They were able to take the first semester off. Tucker and Colleen can do their work on the road."

"I know you miss them, but I'm sure they are making some amazing memories."

Julie smiled. "I do miss them, but I'm thankful for technology. I swear Vivi is getting so big. She starts pre-school when they get back. I can't believe how fast time moves."

Time sure did move fast. Her wedding was coming up soon, and Janine had no idea what it would look like. When she thought about it, her mind went blank. She'd waited her whole life for this day, and she couldn't seem to make a plan.

"Okay, here's that sweetheart neckline. I think you're going to love this one!" The saleswoman, Joyce, was certainly enthusiastic. She probably just wanted Janine to pick a dress and leave the store since she'd been there for two hours already.

"Let's give it a shot," Janine said, annoyed with herself.

DIXIE WALKED up the front steps of Elaine's house. How many times had she walked up these same steps to have coffee with her longtime friend? It had to be hundreds.

Elaine had been there for her when she was diagnosed with Parkinson's disease. Dixie had tried to be there for her when her health had failed a few years ago. She brought food, took her out to lunch and organized tea parties with other local women. Now that Elaine was gone, she felt an emptiness she hadn't expected. They'd been friends for so long, and now Dixie could really feel the hands of time moving. She wasn't getting any younger, that much was sure.

After her conversation with Abigail, she knew she had to do something to get Celeste to agree to stay. This whole idea had been so important to Elaine, and she had to make it work, even if she didn't totally understand why.

She reached up and pulled the heavy iron doorknocker back, letting it go with a loud thud. As she waited, she marveled at the view Elaine had been blessed to have for so many years. In the front yard stood the most massive willow tree. Tourists often stopped to have their picture taken in front of it. On either end of the front porch, you could poke your head around and see the ocean stretching as far as the eye could see behind the house. It was truly a beautiful place. How anyone could say no to such an amazing offer was beyond her.

A woman she could only assume was Celeste answered the door. She was tall and thin, but there was a strength in the way she was standing. Or maybe it was more of a defensive stance. She didn't look particularly welcoming, and stared at Dixie for a moment before crossing her arms.

"And you are?" she finally said.

Dixie knew Abigail was making herself scarce for a few hours so that she would have time to chat with Celeste.

"I know you couldn't possibly remember me, but I was a dear friend of Elaine's. I remember you from when you were a little girl. I'm Dixie." She reached out her hand, and Celeste looked at it for a long moment before finally shaking it.

"What can I do for you, Dixie?"

"Well, I'd like to talk to you, if you don't mind. May I come in?"

She sighed. "Fine. But, I'm getting ready to leave soon to head back to Texas, so you'll have to watch me scarf down a sandwich."

"Not a problem," Dixie said, stepping through the doorway. A blanket of memories washed over her as she smelled the familiar scent of Elaine's home. Always a mixture of coconut and the salty sea air.

Celeste moved past her into the kitchen and sat back down at the table. A half-eaten ham sandwich with a few chips was sitting on a plate. "I'd offer you a sandwich, but we ran out of bread. Want some chips?" She slid a bag of barbecue potato chips toward Dixie.

"No thanks. I had a big breakfast." Dixie sat down and folded her hands in front of her.

"So, are you one of the three friends?"

"Pardon?"

"In the will. The lawyer said Elaine had three friends who would be our judge and jury."

"Well, I hope he didn't put it quite that way. But, yes, I am one of the friends."

"Who are the others?"

"Henrietta and SuAnn."

"How did they know Elaine?"

"Henrietta, much like myself, had been friends with her for decades. SuAnn had only recently met her, but they spent more time together in the last year. Elaine was very involved in local activities and clubs, as I'm sure you know."

Celeste eyed her carefully. "I haven't seen or talked to the woman since I was a kid. Why would I know that?"

Dixie cleared her throat. "I guess I just thought you may remember how she was back then."

"All I remember about Elaine Benson is that she didn't like me very much. She loved

Abigail, and really all the other kids that came and went. But me? Nope."

Dixie smiled. "Celeste, she left you half of a million dollar house on the ocean. Would you leave that to someone you didn't like?"

She popped the last bite of the sandwich into her mouth and stared at her plate. "I have to admit that part makes no sense to me. She had dozens of kids live with her over the years. Why leave it to the one you didn't like?"

"Because she did like you. She loved you. She told me that many times."

"Please don't lie to save my feelings because I honestly don't care." She stood up and put her plate in the sink. "Either way, I can't stay here. I have a life and a job in Texas."

"Do you?"

"Excuse me?"

Dixie stood and leaned against the breakfast bar. "Look, I don't know you very well."

"You don't know me at all."

"Fair enough. But, darlin', pardon me for saying so, but you seem angry."

"I am angry. Do you know my history?"

"I do. Elaine told me a lot about you. She agonized over how to help you back then."

"I don't remember it that way." Celeste turned and rinsed her plate before drying it and putting it back in the cabinet.

"You were a kid, Celeste. Elaine tried so many avenues to get you more counseling and other help. Things were just so limited back then. She was on her knees praying for you every single day."

"Then why did she send me away from here? I was here for two years and then got shipped off to a group home where I stayed until they kicked me out at eighteen years old."

Dixie could see the anger on her face, but she could hear and feel the pain in her voice. Her mother had always told her that anger was just pain and frustration in disguise.

"She didn't kick you out."

"What?"

"My goodness, is that what you've thought all these years?"

"It's true."

"No, it's not. Social services removed you because you kept getting into trouble. Elaine kept asking for help, and instead of providing that help, they removed you. Guess they thought she was rocking the boat too much or couldn't handle you. She cried for weeks after you were taken from her. She truly considered you a daughter, just like Abigail. The two of you were always her favorites."

Celeste stared at her like she had two heads. "I think you have me confused with someone else."

Dixie was growing exasperated. "No, I don't. Somewhere in this house are her journals, and I'm sure she wrote about all of it."

"Well, unfortunately, I won't be here to read them. In fact, I have to get going soon. I have a long drive back to Texas." Celeste started walking toward the front door, a sure sign she wanted to send Dixie on her way.

Thankfully, Dixie fancied herself to be un-
stoppable and stubborn as a mule when she
wanted something.

"Can I ask you one last thing?"

Celeste sighed and rolled her eyes, which
almost made Dixie laugh. She'd seen Celeste
do that dozens of times when she lived with
Elaine. It was her go-to reaction whenever
someone was challenging her.

"Fine. What is it?"

"What is your plan?"

"My plan?"

"Yes, your life plan. I mean, do you just
plan to keep doing manual labor for the rest
of your life?"

"Is there something wrong with people
who do manual labor?" She crossed her
arms, and Dixie wondered if she should pull
back a bit.

"Of course not! But you're not getting
any younger, and surely you have bigger
plans for yourself?"

"Look, I really don't have time for this…"

"Celeste, staying in this house for three

months will change your life. Even if you don't mend fences with Abigail or fall in love with Seagrove, you'll at least walk away with a half million dollars, if not more. Why would you deny yourself this fresh start? When else are you going to have money handed to you on a silver platter like this? I think if you go back to Texas right now, you'll regret it for the rest of your life."

Dixie had found that when all else failed, guilt and greed usually won out. As a mother, she'd learned when to use guilt and when to use greed on her sons. Sometimes, William would need good old mother's guilt to keep him on the straight and narrow. At other times, bribery was the best course of action. Little kids could be greedy when they wanted another piece of candy or a day at the beach.

"Three months is a long time when I have such a big project back home."

"But do you want to do construction? Is that your big dream?"

She looked at the floor and thought for a moment. "Not particularly."

"What is your big dream?"

"I have no idea."

"Everybody has one. Maybe you just haven't allowed yourself to dream."

She shrugged her shoulders. "When you grow up like I did, and you've had to fight for everything you've ever gotten since you were three years old, you learn not to dream."

Dixie's heart ached for her. Celeste was a tough nut to crack, but why wouldn't she be? She'd never been truly loved, and even though Elaine had loved her, Celeste hadn't been able to feel it. Her exterior shell was harder than granite. She wanted to reach out and hug her, but she feared Celeste might clock her right across the face. She was like a caged animal being taunted by little kids at the zoo.

"Don't you think it's time to give yourself some grace? Allow yourself to accept this gift and propel your life forward in the direction you choose to go?" Dixie asked softly.

Celeste stared straight ahead, not making eye contact. She didn't strike Dixie as someone who would ever admit when someone else was right, and Dixie didn't need that. She just needed her to stay so that Elaine would be up in heaven smiling.

"I'll give it some thought."

That was really all Dixie could ask for at this point. "Wonderful. If you need to reach me, here's my cell number." She handed her a small piece of paper where she'd written her contact info, just in case.

Celeste took it and stuck it straight into her pocket. "Thanks."

Dixie said nothing else and let herself out. She figured she'd done all she could do, and now it was up to Celeste.

* * *

CELESTE SAT AT THE TABLE, her phone on speaker mode.

"Wait, so you're not coming back for three months? The project will almost be finished by then."

Telling her boss that she was basically quitting in the middle of their biggest project to date was making her stomach churn. "I'm really sorry, but this is a life-changing opportunity for me."

"That's all well and good, Celeste, but you agreed to work on this development and see it through." Earl Galvin was a tough boss, and she'd always admired that about him. Owner of the development company where she worked, he didn't take any crap from anyone, including her.

"Earl, I don't know what to say."

"You realize you're fired, right? And this means Jim will take over your position. When you come back to Texas, you'll have to start all over."

Yeah, but she'd have half a million dollars to start over with, she thought to herself. Maybe she'd jet set around the world and see all the places she never thought she'd be able to see. Rome, Paris, Scotland, Hawaii. Of course, she'd have to go alone, as usual.

She sucked in a deep breath and slowly allowed it to escape from her nose. "Tell Jim I said congratulations. Thanks for everything, Earl."

Before he could respond, she ended the call and set her phone on the table, her hands folded on the table.

"Everything okay?" Abigail asked as she suddenly appeared in the kitchen. Celeste stood.

"I get the big room with that large tub. I'm taller than you." With that, she brushed past Abigail and walked straight up the stairs.

"HANDS PRESSED TOGETHER at your heart center, and bow your head. Take a long, deep breath in through your nose, hold it… and now blow it slowly out of your lips. And again…"

Janine sat in front of her morning class, her legs crossed. She loved morning classes, but then she was a morning person. All her life, she'd loved seeing the sun come up. A fresh new day, a new opportunity to enjoy the world around her.

"And we bow to each other," she said, smiling as her students opened their eyes. "Namaste."

As the class ended and her students filtered out of the room, she stood in the center, staring at herself in the wall of mirrors. This whole wedding thing was making her nuts.

There were only fleeting moments of her day where she didn't think about her wedding. Janine wasn't one to put so much pressure on herself normally, but for some reason the whole idea of her wedding was overwhelming.

Maybe it was her age. Weddings were meant for young women who had plenty of energy to plan them. A part of her just wanted to run off to the justice of the peace and get it done. She was way more interested in being married than having a wedding.

Another part of her felt like she might regret it if she didn't plan some big event. One of those weddings with a towering cake, five bridesmaids and an adorable flower girl.

She prided herself on knowing who she was. She was very in tune with her inner self. But right now, it felt like she didn't know which end was up. Poor William was just sitting around waiting for her to decide.

"Ready for lunch?"

She turned around to see her friend Emma standing at the entrance of her yoga studio. She hadn't even heard her come in because she'd been so lost in thought.

"Oh, sorry. I didn't realize what time it was. Let me just go grab my bag."

She ran into the other room and retrieved the small backpack she carried with her most of the time. She wasn't one of those women who liked expensive designer handbags. Give her a funky, woven backpack, and she was happy. It didn't take much.

"Is everything okay?" Emma asked.

"Of course. Why do you ask?"

She smiled slightly. "I haven't known you all that long, but you seemed to be a million miles away when I came in."

She and Emma had become good friends after Emma had moved to Seagrove a few months back. She ran the lighthouse, and Janine often liked to spend time at the top of it after it closed. It was a wonderful place to meditate. The views of the marsh at sunset were the most beautiful thing she'd ever seen in her life. The palette of orange and purple had brought her to tears so many times.

"Yeah, I guess I've been guilty of that a lot recently. Just thinking about the wedding."

Emma reached over and squeezed her shoulder. "I feel like you're overthinking this."

"I know I'm overthinking this," Janine said with a laugh.

"Well, why don't we go get some Chinese food and see if we can't put our heads together and figure this out?"

Janine nodded her head. She was so happy to have another good friend in Seagrove. But she wasn't sure that Emma or anyone else was going to be able to figure out what to do about her wedding.

CHAPTER 5

*A*bigail batted at the cobwebs and random spiderwebs as she maneuvered in the small attic space. It was hotter than Satan's house cat, as Elaine used to say. The thought made her smile.

She remembered one time when she had been playing soccer in the yard with some neighborhood kids. It was the middle of July, so she came in all sweaty. Elaine saw her and told her to go take a shower. Abigail had said "Why? Because I'm sweating?" Elaine had smiled and said, "Sweetie, we're southern ladies. We don't sweat. We glisten."

The memories of her time with Elaine always made her smile, but she found herself missing that time in her life. Elaine had loved her, and Abigail had always felt it. She wished she could go back and spend more time with her in the last couple of years. It was something she'd always regret.

"Why is this door open? You're heating up the whole dang house!" Celeste said, popping her head up into the attic.

"If I close it, I'll cook myself like a Thanksgiving turkey."

Celeste made her way up into the space, but she had to hunch over because of her height. The walls were slanted on the sides, and it felt much like going into a tube of some kind. The entire area was stacked with boxes, old rocking chairs, a bassinet, a crib, and many other supplies Elaine had used when taking care of kids for all those years. Why she didn't get rid of this stuff long ago was beyond Abigail. Maybe she thought she would one day take care of kids again.

"What are you doing?"

"Well, since we are the responsible parties for this house and the belongings in it, I thought I'd better go through the stuff so we can clear out the house. After all, it seems like we'll be selling it in three months, right?"

"Right."

"You could help me so this would go faster." She stared at Celeste.

"I actually have a busy day planned."

"Doing what?"

She could see Celeste trying to come up with a valid reason for getting out of the hot attic. "Okay, fine. But we can't stay up here. Let's grab some boxes and go downstairs."

Abigail couldn't really argue, given that she was quickly dehydrating and becoming a little delirious. "Here, take these two boxes and I'll grab these bags over here."

For the next half hour, they went up and down the attic stairs, taking box after box. Celeste also took the baby stuff and rocking chairs and put them in the unused formal dining room. They planned to give any of the usable stuff to the local thrift store and take the rest to the local dump.

When all was said and done, they sat in the living room surrounded by boxes and bags. Abigail was hesitant to open them, feeling like she was invading Elaine's privacy, but it had to be done. She refused to throw anything away that might be important.

Without speaking, they each started digging through boxes. Most of the papers were old documents about her time in the foster care system. Some were letters from previous kids, others were notes from thankful charities that she'd supported over the years. Elaine had truly made the most of her life.

"This box is just full of old books. We can donate these," Celeste said unemotionally.

"Let me see those."

"Why?"

"Because I might want something in there." She held her hands out, ready to take the box.

"You don't trust me, do you?"

Abigail paused a moment. "No, but that has nothing to do with why I want to look in that box. Now give it to me."

Celeste stood and dropped it at her feet, barely missing her toes. She sucked in a deep breath and willed herself not to snap. She wouldn't stoop to Celeste's level. She refused.

They continued working in silence for a while. Abigail preferred silence to arguing. Even with her ex-husband, she did anything she could to keep the peace. Confrontation was her least favorite thing in the world, which was why living with Celeste again was going to be the greatest challenge she'd ever faced.

"This box is just old bank statements from like twenty years ago. Why did she keep all this crap that we now have to deal with?" She emptied the box's contents into the trash bag and picked up the next one.

"I guess she just thought she'd get to all of it later. We never know when our time is up."

Celeste reached into the next box and

stopped, staring down into it for a moment. "I think these are some of her journals."

"Journals? I didn't know she kept journals."

"Dixie told me."

She watched the look on Celeste's face as she was obviously trying to decide whether to look at them or pretend she didn't care. In the end, she pushed the box aside and chose to pretend. Abigail opted not to push. She'd find some time to look at them later.

"Should we go get another load?" Abigail asked as they finished what they'd brought down.

"No. I'll take this trash and the stuff nobody will want over to the dump. I should be able to fit it in my truck."

"Okay. I'll clean this up and maybe see if the bookstore wants this box of books for their used books section."

Celeste didn't say another word and started gathering up the trash. Something about those journals was obviously triggering her, but Abigail knew better than to push her.

* * *

JULIE SET the basket of rolls in the middle of the table. Lucy had taken a week off to go visit family in Louisiana, so she was on her own preparing this dinner for Dawson's friend.

Dawson had taken Dylan to Tae Kwon Do, and he would go home with a friend for dinner. Julie thought it was better that way so that she and Dawson would have plenty of time to chat with Ben. Dylan, God love him, would overtake the conversation talking about dinosaurs and the crabs he found down at the shore. Definitely not thrilling dinner party conversation for adults.

"I'm back!" Dawson called as he walked through the front door. He breezed into the dining room, kissed Julie on the head, and looked down at the table. "What can I do?"

That was one of the things she loved most about him. He was always ready to pitch in, and nothing around the house was considered "woman's work". Dawson was a pretty good cook, neat and tidy, and he was always most likely to help Dylan with his homework at night.

"Nothing, really. The only thing left is to get the pitcher of sweet tea out of the refrigerator, but we can do that right before Ben gets here."

"Sounds good. I'm really excited to see him. I can't believe it's been so many years."

"Do you know what he's been doing all these years?"

"Believe it or not, he's a pediatrician."

"Wow, so a very smart guy. Maybe he can explain to us why Dylan is smelling that way."

Dawson laughed. "Oh, my dear, it's only the beginning. Wait until he's actually a teenager."

"I'm going to need some kind of gas mask then," Julie said, chuckling. She loved her son, but boys were dirty. Boys could be gross. Maybe she had been spoiled by raising two little girls who only wanted to be princesses. Dylan would not become a prince anytime soon.

There was a knock at the door, and Julie felt a bit nervous. Meeting one of Dawson's oldest friends had her a bit on edge. There was a part of her that wanted people to like her, and she didn't like that part of herself. She wanted to be like Dixie and not give one wit what somebody thought of her, but maybe she would grow into that as she got older.

Dawson walked into the living room and opened the door. Julie stood back in the doorway of the dining room and watched him greet his old friend after decades apart. After exchanging some pleasantries, hand-shakes, and a hug, Dawson turned around with a broad smile.

"Ben, I want you to meet my wife, Julie."

Julie walked forward and reached out her hand. She was surprised at how tall Ben was.

He had to be at least six-foot-three, possibly more. Her natural inclination was always to ask tall people if they ever played basketball until one of her old friends told her that tall people got really sick of that question. Still, she always wondered about it in her head.

"So nice to meet you finally," she said, shaking his hand. "Dawson has told me some wonderful things about you. You're a pediatrician, right?"

He smiled. "I am. I've been practicing for about fifteen years now."

"That's wonderful. I'm sure working with kids all day can be a little exhausting."

"Definitely, but it's worth it. Although I will say I'm always tired at the end of the day."

"Well, I know you've had a long trip, so why don't you come into the dining room and have a seat? We can take your bags up to your room after we eat if that's okay with you?"

"Of course. Plus, I'm famished. That was a long ride."

He followed her into the dining room, with Dawson trailing behind him. Dawson went straight into the kitchen to get the pitcher of tea while Julie sat down with Ben across from her.

"So Dawson tells me you are the co-owner of a bookstore here in town?"

She nodded her head. "Yes, it's just a small little place that I own with a friend of mine. It's called Down Yonder Books. I didn't name the place, but I think it's cute."

He nodded his head. "It seems very fitting for this area. It's been so many years since I've been back in Seagrove. I can't believe how it's changed, but how it hasn't at the same time. Not sure if that makes any sense."

"I only moved here fairly recently, so I wouldn't know what it was like when you were kids. It immediately felt like home to me. I can't imagine living anywhere else."

Dawson reappeared in the dining room with a pitcher of tea. "Sweet tea, I assume?"

"We're in the south, so I think it's a law," Ben said, laughing.

As Dawson poured the tea, Julie passed the plate of pork roast toward Ben. She definitely wasn't as good a cook as Lucy, but she'd made the roast, green beans, mashed potatoes and even a peach cobbler for dessert. Thank goodness Lucy had left her some written recipes for when she was on vacation. She was pretty sure she thought they might all die of starvation if she didn't leave some kind of instructions.

Once they had all put food on their plates, Julie started eating to allow Dawson and Ben some time to catch up.

"Are you happy to be back in Seagrove?" Dawson asked.

"It's definitely different. I loved living in Denver, but after the divorce there were just too many memories there."

"Do your parents still live in Seagrove?" Julie asked.

Ben dabbed at his mouth with the cloth napkin and shook his head. "No. My father passed away when I was in high school, and my mother lives with my stepfather in Virginia now. He works for a big defense contractor up there."

"Will you open an office here? Seagrove could use a new pediatrician. Ever since old Dr. Willard died, we haven't had one," Dawson said before taking a bite of his mashed potatoes.

"I'd like to. Is his office space still available?"

"Actually, no. An accountant snatched it up before they could even have a funeral for the old man. It's hard to find commercial space here, you know. Everybody stays forever."

"I may have to move closer to Charleston then. Have to make a living," he said, taking a sip of his tea.

"Do you have any kids, Ben?"

He shook his head. "No, I don't. My wife... ex-wife, I mean... couldn't have kids. She had a cancer scare in her early twenties and had to have a hysterectomy."

"Oh wow. That's terrible."

"We were married for almost twenty years."

"I got divorced after twenty-one years. It was a very difficult time in my life."

He smiled. "And then you met my pal, Dawson, huh?"

"Best thing that ever happened to me," she said, reaching over and squeezing Dawson's hand.

"Oh, I'm not interested in going down that road again. I think it's best to focus on my work for a while."

"You never know when love might sneak up and bite you again," Julie said, pouring more tea into his glass.

"Well, they do say love bites," he joked.

Julie wanted everyone to find the happiness she'd found. When she was going through the breakup of her marriage, she never imagined how much better life could be. Sometimes a person had to go through the darkest times to find the light.

* * *

ABIGAIL WALKED ALONG THE SURF, allowing it to wash over her feet. There was nothing quite as relaxing as being near the ocean. She had missed it so much over the years. Of course, as a kid, she had no idea how blessed she was to be able to walk out her back door and be on the beach.

She hadn't lived with Elaine for that long, but those two years made more of an impression on her than much of her other years combined. There were so many times that she wished she could've been adopted by Elaine, although she loved her adoptive parents. It just wasn't the same. She had had a connection with Elaine that she never forged with her adoptive mother.

Being back in Seagrove was stirring up all kinds of memories. She wished that she had a family of her own she could share these moments with. After her marriage ended, she had never felt such a sense of failure.

When she and Danny had first married, they had all the dreams of every newly married couple. Grow their careers, buy a beautiful home, have children. They were able to accomplish the first one, but the next two never happened.

Danny had wanted to be a father almost from the moment they met, but Abigail couldn't conceive. No matter what she tried, no matter how many treatments she went through, it just wasn't happening. It created cracks in the marriage, so they started going to counseling.

Unfortunately for Abigail, then he fell in love with the receptionist at their counselor's office. She certainly didn't see that coming.

After their divorce was final, he immediately married her, and she was pregnant within a few weeks. Abigail didn't like to admit that she had spied on his Facebook page a few times, but as soon as she saw the pictures from their ultrasound, she opted to delete the app to keep herself from feeling tempted. It didn't serve her to look at those pictures. It only made her miserable. It only made her feel like more of a failure.

When Celeste asked her what she had done with her life, it had hit her hard. As much as she wished she had done some really important things, all she had really done was work in a field that didn't excite her and marry a man who didn't love her.

And now here she was, back in Seagrove. Somehow, they had to decide on what to do with the house. How in the world was she going to work with a woman who was so difficult? How would they ever come up with something they could agree on?

JANINE STOOD at the top of the lighthouse, staring out over the marsh and the ocean beyond. This was one of her favorite places on earth, and today she needed the escape.

Emma had unlocked the door and allowed her to spend some time at the top, meditating and doing her nightly yoga stretches. She needed to clear her mind and figure out why she was struggling so hard with what to do for her wedding.

There were moments she thought maybe she was questioning her marriage to William, but she quickly realized that wasn't the case. She loved him more than anyone she had ever loved in her life. He was her rock, her best friend. There was nothing about getting married to him she was questioning.

But she was feeling this pressure to create the perfect wedding. Maybe it was because she had waited so long to get married she felt like the buildup was huge. Maybe she was trying to compare herself to other people she knew who had gotten married. What did it say about her if she didn't want a great big wedding? Was her marriage any less real because she wasn't excited about putting on a white dress and dragging a mile-long train?

She gazed out over the marsh, watching a large, old turtle amble over a thick piece of wood. Something about staring out over the mixture of life and death that inhabited the marsh made her feel peaceful and calm.

The door leading to the top of the lighthouse closed behind her, and she turned to see Emma standing there holding a bottle of wine in one hand and two glasses in the other.

"Ready to relax after a long day?" she asked, smiling. Janine nodded. She opened the two folding chairs that Emma kept at the top of the lighthouse for just this sort of occasion.

They both sat down, and Emma poured each of them a glass of wine. Janine took a sip, and then held it in her mouth for a few moments, closing her eyes. She wasn't a big drinker, but there was nothing better than a great glass of wine after an exhausting day.

"How many classes did you teach today?"

"Six. It was crazy. I'm going to have to adjust my schedule, or I just might die. How many tours did you do?"

"Seven. And one of them was to a huge

class of fifth graders who seemed to be on methamphetamines or something."

"Show off."

Emma laughed. "Your job is a lot more physical than mine. All I have to do is go up and down the stairs a few times a day. You have to twist your body into all kinds of weird shapes."

"I'm actually kind of a fraud. Most of the time, I just show them the pose and then leisurely walk around the classroom, making sure they're doing it correctly. It's a good way to distract from the fact that I'm not doing all the poses with them."

"I still need to come try out a class again. That first one almost scared me away forever."

"Emma, that was my class for people over sixty. You should've been able to do that easily," Janine said, chuckling.

"Don't make me feel worse than I already do."

"I'm not nearly as stressed out about my classes as I am about this wedding. I don't know why this thing has me so tied up in knots."

"Are you trying to say that you're not sure about tying the knot?" Emma laughed at her own pun.

"Hilarious. But I'm serious. The wedding is coming up in a few weeks, and I have no idea what to put on the invitation because I don't know where I want to get married or what I want to wear…"

"Okay, I have an idea. Let's play a game."

Janine stared at her. "I don't really have time to play Monopoly right now because I'm trying to figure out my wedding." She took another long sip of her wine.

"Not that kind of game, silly. When I was a kid, one of my teachers taught me this. She said that usually your first answer is correct. I kept failing tests because I would put down the right answer but then second-guess my-self until I changed it."

"So what's the game?"

"I'm going to ask you a question and I want you to answer with the first thought that comes into your mind. No judging it, no editing it. No answering what you think someone else might want you to answer. Okay?"

"Fine. I'm willing to try anything at this point."

"First question. If you could be any animal, what would it be?"

Janine furrowed her eyebrows. "How is that supposed to help me with my wedding?"

Emma sighed. "Just trust the process and answer the questions. And you have to be quick."

Janine set her wineglass on the wooden decking and turned so she was facing Emma. "I'm ready."

"Well, I have to change the question now that you know it. New question. What's your favorite color?"

"Blue."

"What's your favorite kind of music?"

"Classic rock."

"Really? I thought it would be something like classical or that spa music."

"Excuse me, but I don't think you get to judge my answers."

Emma giggled. "You're right, but we're coming back to that whole classic rock thing. Next question, do you want a fancy wedding dress?"

"No." Janine sat there for a moment, her eyes wide. "Wait. Did I just say no?"

Emma nodded. "You sure did. You definitely do not want to wear a fancy wedding dress."

"Wow. I've been agonizing over that decision for weeks now. "

"Let's keep going. What's your favorite animal?"

"Dogs."

"What's your favorite scent?"

"Coffee."

"Where do you want to get married?"

"At the top of the lighthouse." Again, Janine's eyes widened. "At the lighthouse?" she repeated slowly.

"You want to get married here? At the top of the lighthouse?"

Janine smiled. "Is that crazy?"

"A little. I mean, I've never rented this place out for a wedding, and I'm not sure how that would work with guests or a wedding party..."

"I don't think I want any guests."

"No guests?"

"Just close friends and family. Julie, my mom, my nieces, Dixie, you, the guys. Do you think we could fit everyone up here?"

Emma looked around. "As long as nobody gains any more weight between now and then."

Janine laughed. "I know it's crazy, but I just realized that this place feels so right to me. I'm the most peaceful here. Ever since I moved to Seagrove, I've been looking for my place that I could go and feel close to God. To the universe. A lot of the times I feel that way at the beach, but not like I do here."

Emma reached over and took both of her hands. "Then you're going to have your wedding right here at the top of the lighthouse, and I am going to help you make that happen."

"Well, I think I better start with seeing if William is willing to get married up here. For all I know, he wants to have a giant wedding in a church. What if he doesn't want to have the wedding up here?"

Emma smiled. "Janine, he adores you. I don't think he cares where you get married as long as you get married."

CHAPTER 6

*C*eleste leaned back against the wooden headboard. She didn't remember this room being so large. Being in Elaine's old bedroom didn't bring back a lot of memories, since she had spent little time in there as a kid. Elaine treated her bedroom like a sanctuary, which wasn't overly surprising given that she always had a plethora of kids in her house. Celeste really couldn't blame her for that.

She stared out the window at the ocean. It was sunset, but the most beautiful skies were seen over the marsh. Still, there were hints of pink and orange streaking across the sky as the water got darker and darker under the disappearing remnants of daylight.

She was procrastinating. There was no question about that. After all, the stack of journals sitting beside her were taunting her, calling her name. She was quite sure that when she started reading those journals, she would find out exactly what Elaine really thought about her. After all, people were much less likely to lie in their own private journals.

Dixie could say whatever she wanted, but Celeste knew Elaine didn't like her. She was treated differently from the moment she arrived at the house. Left to her own devices most of the time, she saw the way Elaine had doted on Abigail. At the time, it probably hurt her feelings, but she was not likely to admit it.

Celeste was well aware that she was a tough nut to crack. At times, it was difficult to keep up the façade of being the strongest person in the room at any given time. But she'd lived this way since she was three years old. Or at least she assumed so. She couldn't remember back that far.

A lot of kids could remember things from a very young age, but Celeste didn't. She assumed there was trauma in her past and her brain wasn't allowing her to access it. For that, she was grateful.

She knew little about her birth mother other than the fact that she was a teenager when she had her. From what Celeste had been told, she attempted to keep her, but when she was just two weeks past her third birthday, her mother took her to the fire station and told her to sit on the front steps.

The story that Celeste was told was that her mother gave her a teddy bear and promised her she would be back in a few minutes. She said that she just needed to sit there for a little while until a nice firefighter found her.

Of course, Celeste couldn't remember any of that. All she knew was that the woman who gave birth to her and was supposed to love her for the rest of her life left her. It wasn't like she was a newborn that didn't have a personality yet. She was three years old. Her mother knew her better than anyone, and she still left her. Abandoned her. Gave her to strangers.

She reached over and picked up the first journal. She had no idea if they were in any particular order. Celeste had waited until Abigail went to bed just so she didn't ask her any questions about why she was reading those journals. She figured she would read what she wanted to read and slip them back into the box before Abigail knew they were gone.

Sighing as she leaned back against the bed, she opened the first one. From the dates, she could tell that it was when she had been at the house for about a month.

Celeste is a difficult child, no matter how hard I try to make her feel welcome. She's combative, defiant and often blurts out vulgarities.

That made Celeste giggle. When she was a kid, she was always trying to get a reaction out of people, and one way she found to do that was to say inappropriate things at inappropriate times.

She continued reading the first journal, which was mostly notes about Elaine's frustrations with the foster system, working with a particularly difficult social worker and detailing all the children in her care at that time.

It appeared she had five kids living with her off and on during the two years that Celeste was there. Of course, Celeste remembered Abigail very well, but her memories of the other kids were pretty hazy.

From Elaine's notes, she had a newborn, a three-year-old and a six-year-old. Celeste had memories of the infant crying at night, and she had some memories of Christmas with little kids running around, but that was about it.

Celeste and Abigail fight like cats and dogs. While Abigail is a very fragile, shy little girl, Celeste is most certainly not. She's boisterous, loud, and opinionated even for her age. The times I have tried to put her in her place, she has pushed back with a force unlike any I've ever seen.

So far, everything she had read about herself in Elaine's journals had lined up with what she thought was Elaine's opinion of her. She only wrote down the most negative things, but Celeste was sure that she had done some positive things during those two years.

She hadn't been the best student, but she did manage to win the science fair one of those years. Of course, she cheated off the smartest girl in class and basically stole her idea, but she won. In fact, she still had that blue ribbon somewhere in her keepsake boxes.

She closed up the first journal and tossed it across the bed before picking up the next one. Each one was leather bound in basically the same drab brown color. Some were more worn than others, and one had what appeared to be droplets of water stain on the covers.

She opened the next journal to see some drawings. She had no idea that Elaine liked to draw, but she was pretty talented. The drawings were mostly of flowers, many of them similar to the ones that she had in her garden back in those days.

There were even a couple of landscapes with the ocean and sunrises in the background. She had colored those in with colored pencils and scattered them throughout her journal.

It was interesting that she could tell what kind of day Elaine was having by what she was drawing. Was it a picture of a dark tree with gray skies? Or a beautiful vine of roses, vibrant in color?

Today, Celeste told me she hated me. We were just sitting at the dinner table, having meatloaf, when she glared at me. I told her that wasn't appropriate behavior at the dinner table and she said she hated me. I excused myself, using the excuse that I needed to use the restroom, and I cried. But I can't let her see that she's gotten to me because a child who thinks she's in control will never learn discipline or feel loved. The tears are still falling as I write this, droplets staining the front cover of this journal. Why can't I get through to this child? I want her to feel what love is, but I can't find a way to get through to her.

Celeste stared at the paper for a moment. She felt a twinge of guilt. Elaine had gone to the bathroom to cry? She hadn't expected that. As tough as Celeste was, Elaine seemed tougher at the time. She never showed her cards. She didn't even remember the incident Elaine was writing about.

Celeste got in trouble at school again today. Her teacher called and said that if I couldn't get her under control, they will have to send her to a special school for troublemakers. I can't have that happen. I know she's a good kid underneath all of that rough exterior. I'm not giving up on her.

She quickly closed the journal and stared at it, her hand shaking a bit as she set it to the side. Elaine had said she would not give up on her. Did she actually care about her?

Celeste was starting to wonder if Dixie was right. Maybe her immature young mind had misjudged this woman who was trying to help her.

She couldn't look at the journals anymore tonight. It had been a lot harder than she thought it would be to go back in time. Maybe she would do it tomorrow. For now, she slid them into a drawer in her nightstand and turned off the lamp. Lying in the complete darkness with only the light of the moon coming through the window, she felt a heaviness wash over her chest.

This was going to be a long three months.

ABIGAIL WALKED DOWN THE STREET, passing all the different businesses. There were so many places she wanted to check out, like the hair salon, the bakery, and maybe even the yoga studio. She was looking forward to enjoying her time in Seagrove, even if it only lasted for three months.

She was a planner. Not knowing exactly what her life was going to look like after three months was driving her crazy already. But pushing Celeste to make any longer commitment than that was futile. The woman was already on edge most of the time, and she was afraid if she said much to her about what would happen after the three months, that Celeste would just take off in the middle of the night.

A big part of her hoped she could keep the house and somehow buy out Celeste, but she knew she didn't have the money to do that. In all likelihood, they would have to sell the place, and Abigail would walk away with over half a million dollars, leaving all of her memories behind.

She decided not to think that far ahead, but instead go into the little bookstore on the square. And she opened the door, a bell dinged loudly and the woman behind the counter smiled.

"Welcome to Down Yonder Books. I'm Julie. How can I help you?"

The place was cute, with a small café and all sorts of coffee and muffins available. It was like an old-time bookstore, a great place to get away from the modern world, full of noise and electronics.

"I'm Abigail. I just thought I'd take a look around, if you don't mind."

"You're Abigail? The one who inherited Elaine Benson's house?"

She nodded. "Well, I inherited half of it. The other half belongs to another foster child she had named Celeste."

Julie laughed. "Oh yes, Dixie told me all about Celeste."

"I can't imagine what she told you, but just take whatever she said and triple it. It's *that* bad."

Julie walked out from behind the counter and pointed at one of the bistro tables. "Why don't you have a seat and we'll have a cup of coffee and chat about it?"

Abigail sat down and waited while Julie went back behind the counter to make the coffee. This was what small towns were like.

They were places you could sit down with a new friend, have a cup of coffee and chat about life.

She'd had enough of big cities. She'd been dreaming about living in a place like Seagrove for many years. No matter what happened with the house, maybe she would end up staying here. Maybe she could make a new life here away from the hustle and bustle.

Taking a leave of absence from her job in public relations had been an easy decision. She was highly qualified and very good at what she did, so her boss had no problem allowing her to take that short break. The question was, would she ever go back?

"Cream and sugar?"

"Both, please. When I make coffee, I like it to look like an off-white wall before I drink it."

Julie chuckled as she walked over to the table and put two coffees down with a small creamer pitcher and a bowl of sugar cubes.

"I know what you mean. I don't even think mine is actually coffee anymore."

"Thank you. This is very good," Abigail said after taking a sip.

"So, you lived in Seagrove when you were a kid?"

"Just for a couple of years. I wish I could've stayed here forever."

"I only moved here a short time ago myself. It's the best place on earth as far as I'm concerned. I've been able to create my dream life here."

Abigail nodded. "I can see how that would be the case. Seagrove is special."

"That it is. So, from what Dixie tells me, you and Celeste had a bit of a difficult history together?"

"True, but that's mainly because Celeste is difficult all by herself. She's had a troubled past. She was left at a fire station at three years old by her mother. It has really affected her."

A look of empathy washed over Julie's face. "Wow. That's terrible. I can't imagine how that would affect a child to be left like that. I mean, three years old? I could never imagine giving up my child at that age. I mean, she knew her. She had to have developed a bond with Celeste by then."

"Yes, and I think it still affects her today. It's not like her mother took her to an adoption agency. She just abandoned her. Anyway, Celeste is tough. She can be very abrasive, and she is definitely stubborn as a mule."

"We adopted a little boy recently. He's the light of our lives. His name is Dylan." Julie pulled up a picture on her phone and showed it to Abigail. There was a cute little boy holding a fish on a line with a big grin on his face.

"He's adorable. Adoption is a wonderful thing."

"He was in foster care after his father, who had addiction problems, passed away. We actually met Dylan when we hosted a camp. We own The Inn at Seagrove, and we hosted a foster kid camp. My husband just fell in love with him."

"A foster kid camp? What a unique idea. We had nothing like that when I was a kid. Celeste ended up in foster care her whole life."

"Really? She was never adopted?"

"No. She really got a raw deal from the time she was three years old, and probably before. Part of me feels sorry for her, but she's so hard to be close to."

"I can't imagine never having parents to guide you and being passed around from foster home to foster home your whole life. And then they just throw you out into the world and expect you to do well."

"Celeste isn't a very talkative, open person, so I don't know how she taught herself to be an adult. But she has done pretty well, I think. She was managing the development of a new subdivision in Texas before she came here."

They continued chatting and drinking their coffee for quite some time. Abigail really enjoyed having someone to talk to in Seagrove. Living at the house with Celeste was quiet and uncomfortable.

"So I understand you and Celeste have to come to an agreement on how you'll use the house?"

"Yeah, and we're not exactly the best at negotiating with each other."

"Do you have any idea what you want to do?"

Abigail shook her head. "No ideas at all. It's such a big house, and I'm sure it could be put to good use for something, but I have no idea what it is."

"Do you have any particular causes that are close to your heart?"

"Well, of course I feel very strongly about foster care and adoption."

"That makes sense. Maybe you can have some kind of camp like we did."

Abigail thought for a moment. "It's a good idea, but we're being judged by Dixie and two other friends of Elaine's. I don't think copying your foster care camp is going to get us there."

Julie laughed. "Those other two women are Henrietta, whose husband is the mayor of town, and my mother, SuAnn."

"Your mother?"

"Yeah, it's kind of weird, but she and Elaine forged a friendship during the last year or so. Dixie introduced them."

"So what do you think about our judges? Are we going to have an easy time convincing them?"

Julie shook her head and chuckled. "Out of all the women I know in Seagrove, those three are going to take the most effort to impress. They're pretty stubborn old birds. Don't tell them I said old, though."

Abigail was feeling more worried by the minute. How in the world was she going to work closely with Celeste for three months and impress the women who knew Elaine best?

"Well, I guess I had better think of some options. I really would like to do something related to foster care. Do you have any contacts there, by chance?"

Julie nodded her head and got up, retrieving her purse from behind the counter. She pulled out her wallet and dug through it before finally finding what she was looking for.

"Here's the card for one woman we work with over there. She does some follow-up with us from time to time, and we're planning another camp next summer."

Abigail took the card and slipped it into her pocket. "Thank you so much. I will definitely talk to Celeste, or at least I'll try to. Do you mind if I take a look around? I might want to pick up a few books to read down by the beach."

"Of course. And if I can ever do anything to help you, I'm here. That's how Seagrove works. We all help each other."

Abigail smiled gratefully before she headed toward the back of the store to look at some of the mystery books she'd noticed when she walked in. She was looking for something to read that would whisk her away out of her current circumstance of trying to live with Celeste. Unfortunately, she wasn't sure there was a book on the planet that would distract her from that.

CHAPTER 7

*C*eleste walked up and down the streets on the square, trying to reacquaint herself with the city of Seagrove. It had been so many years since she'd been there, and she really had paid little attention to the businesses that dotted the streets when she was a kid.

She saw a yoga studio, a bakery, a bookstore. She saw the dry cleaners, the hair salon, and a couple of other mom and pop shops. Every single space appeared to be full, which was surprising given that Seagrove wasn't exactly a hotbed of activity.

She remembered the marshes, and she knew there was an island just off the coast. Someone had told her there was an inn there now. Other than that, Seagrove didn't have a bunch of big box stores.

Right now, she just needed to find the small grocery store she was told was just off the square. It didn't seem like Abigail was an avid cook, so the responsibility of keeping the refrigerator and pantry stocked seemed to be falling on her. Tonight, she was planning on grilling some steaks and popping a couple of baked potatoes in the oven.

She was feeling like a fifties housewife, cooking dinner for her husband after he came home from a long day at work. The only difference was that she was cooking for her arch nemesis, who appeared to just be out meeting people and having fun while she figured out how both of them would continue to eat.

She turned down Sawgrass Street, finally seeing the grocery store up ahead on the left side of the road. Looking down, she noticed that one of her shoes was untied, so she stopped to bend down and tie it.

Just as she did, someone or something barreled into the side of her body, knocking her over. She narrowly missed falling over the edge of the curb. She could have fallen into oncoming traffic if there was any traffic at all in Seagrove.

"What on earth?" she yelled, immediately sitting up and grabbing her elbow, which was now scraped. She felt like a little kid who fell off her bicycle.

"Oh, my gosh! I'm so sorry. Here, let me help you up." She heard a man's voice, but when she tried to look up, the bright sunlight obscured her view. All she could see was the silhouette of someone who was taller than she was, which was a very hard thing to find.

"Let go of me!" she shouted as he pulled on her other arm. He immediately let go, his hands up in front of him. Slowly, she ambled up onto her feet, brushing off the front of her jeans. Even though it was hot, she was used to wearing jeans at work. It was a good thing or else she would've skinned up both of her legs.

Now her favorite blue T-shirt had a small rip in the shoulder from the force of falling down. She would make this guy pay for that.

"I'm sorry. I didn't see you there."

She could finally look him in the face, and it required her to look upward a bit. He wasn't much taller than she was, maybe four or five inches, but it was very unusual for her to find someone that could match her stature. Although right now his shoulders were hunching forward, probably because he was completely embarrassed for knocking her over.

"I'm not sure how you could miss me. I'm almost six feet tall and I was simply tying my shoe. You obviously weren't looking where you were going!"

"You're right."

Celeste wasn't used to people taking responsibility so easily.

"I'm right?"

He smiled. It was one of those lazy smiles where only one side of the corner of his mouth went up. And there was a smile line, right next to a dimple. And he had a southern drawl that she wasn't expecting by the way he dressed so professionally. His voice sounded like he should wear a cowboy hat.

"Look, I'm really sorry. The truth is, I saw a dog."

She stared at him. "And you've never seen a dog before?"

He laughed. "Yes, I've seen a dog. But this one was particularly cute, and I guess I got distracted."

She took a deep breath and blew it out slowly, forcing herself not to say anything too antagonistic. After all, he had admitted fault, and he was good looking enough that she was willing to let him have a pass.

"Well, try to keep yourself focused next time. I'd hate for you to walk right out into traffic," she said, trying to make a joke as she looked down the road. As far as flirting went, Celeste was quite rusty. She hadn't dated anyone in a couple of years, mostly because she was fiercely independent and many men didn't appreciate that quality in her.

"I'll try. I'm Ben, by the way." He reached his hand out to shake hers, and she reluctantly took it. His hands weren't overly soft, but they weren't rough either. She figured he probably worked in an office somewhere.

"Celeste."

"Are you from around here?"

"I went to school here for a couple of years, but I haven't been back in decades."

"Same. I also went to school here and left just before ninth grade. Maybe we passed each other in the halls?"

"No offense, but I think you're a little older than me."

There she went, sticking her foot squarely in her mouth. But he didn't flinch at all and smiled.

"You're probably right. Well, it was nice running into you."

Celeste couldn't help but laugh at his lame attempt at a joke. "Funny. Not so nice running into you." She looked at her elbow and pulled at her ripped T-shirt.

"Why don't you let me walk over to the drugstore and get you a bandage? And I'm happy to buy you a new shirt…"

She waved her hand at him. "I work in the construction field. I'm used to getting hurt and damaging my clothing. No biggie."

He looked a bit surprised when she admitted she worked in construction. There weren't many women in the world who could say that.

"Here, at least let me give you some pain and suffering money," he said, attempting to hand her a twenty-dollar bill. "Sorry, that's all the cash I have on me right now."

She furrowed her eyebrows, looking up at him. "It's okay, really. But I do have to go. Grocery shopping, you know."

He nodded his head. "Good luck with that. I think I'll take a different route home. Maybe I'll see another dog."

As he wandered off, Celeste watched him walk, hoping he didn't turn around and catch her. She hadn't seen a man that handsome in a very long time, although most men certainly didn't find her to be of interest. She was rough around the edges, and she was proud of it. It would take a very strong man to be with her, which was why she had spent so much of her life alone.

* * *

"AT THE TOP OF THE LIGHTHOUSE?" William looked at her like she had just said she wanted to build a house on the moon.

"I know it sounds crazy, but I love being up there."

He sat down on the edge of the dock beside her. Janine often came down to see him at the end of a long day. It was a beautiful place to watch the sunset.

"Janine, I know you love the lighthouse, and I think that's great. But how in the world are we supposed to have all of these people at the top? It's not that big, and it's curved. At best, we could probably get ourselves and the minister up there."

"Emma said that the doors open to the gallery."

"The gallery?"

"The glass enclosed room. We should be able to get some chairs in there and we could stand just in the doorway with the minister. I think it would work. Plus, the platform is pretty large for a lighthouse. I thought we could cut our guest list down to just our closest friends and family, and then maybe have a bigger reception somewhere else."

He sat for a moment and stared off over the water. She wondered if he felt like she was hijacking their wedding and not allowing him to have any input. The last thing she wanted was for William to feel like he didn't get the wedding he wanted, too.

"William, say something. If you don't like the idea…"

He smiled. "You're unique, Janine."

"What?"

"When we first met, you got under my skin because you were so different, and I couldn't figure out how to interact with you. I mean, here's this beautiful woman who contorts her body in these weird ways, burns incense and meditates. I was the guy who worked all the time and had lost who he was. Now, I own this fishing charter business, and I love my life."

"Okay, but what about the lighthouse?"

He looked at her. "Don't you see?"

"See what?"

"I know every day being married to you is going to be interesting, and I would expect nothing less of our wedding."

"So we can get married at the top of the lighthouse?"

He smiled. "If you're sure we can fit our crew of people, and that's what you want, then that's what I want."

Janine hugged him tightly. "Really?"

"Really," he said, laughing.

"But, William, I don't want you to think I'm railroading you into this…"

He put his index finger against her lips. "If I ever feel like you're railroading me, I'll speak up. Our wedding day is going to be the best day of my life, but the location doesn't matter to me. You can wear a mermaid costume, have folk singers playing banjos and hire a belly dancer to perform the ceremony. I don't care as long as I get to slip that wedding ring on your finger and call you my wife."

Janine grinned so big that her face hurt. Strangely, that was the most romantic thing anyone had ever said to her. How did she get *this* lucky?

* * *

"So HE KNOCKED you to the ground?" Abigail said, staring at Celeste as she pulled the bandage off her elbow to check the wound.

"It's no big deal. I've gotten hurt worse falling off my motorcycle."

"You have a motorcycle?"

"I did. Back in Texas. Where my life is."

"I think we have some hydrogen peroxide in the medicine cabinet upstairs."

Celeste turned and looked at her. "I'm okay. I'm not a baby. I get hurt all the time on job sites."

"Insurance companies must love you then," Abigail mumbled under her breath. She walked over to the refrigerator and surveyed what they had to cook for dinner.

Living with Celeste as her roommate wasn't something she ever expected to happen in her life. She definitely wouldn't have chosen her, but for some reason, Elaine did. This was just one in a string of tests that life was apparently throwing at her.

"I got the stuff to cook spaghetti," Celeste said matter-of-factly as she sat down at the breakfast table.

"Oh, good. Did you get garlic bread?"

"In the freezer," she said, staring down at her phone.

"You know, at some point we have to discuss what we're going to do with this place."

"I know."

"We only have three months to get it up and running and prove to the committee of three that we've done something good. So, should we have a chat about this?"

"Do you have any ideas?" Celeste asked, looking up.

"Just some general ones. What about you?"

"Not really. I've been so busy grocery shopping and taking things to the thrift store that I haven't had a lot of time to think about it."

"Well, it's all I've been thinking about."

"Figures," Celeste said quietly, although Abigail heard her loud and clear.

"I was thinking maybe we could do something with the foster care system."

Celeste stopped what she was doing, put her phone on the table and stared at Abigail like she had just suggested they form a singing group.

"You've got to be kidding me."

"What's so wrong with that? We both

know that the foster care system needs all the help it can get."

Abigail walked over to the counter and leaned against it, waiting to hear Celeste's response.

"When I left the foster care system, that was the last I ever wanted to see of it. Do you think I want to have a bunch of foster kids living here?"

"No, that's not what I mean. I met this woman. She and her husband own an inn over on the island. They have a camp for foster kids…"

"First, I don't want to run a camp. Little sweaty children running all over the place driving me crazy? No, thank you. And second, I'm pretty sure that we can't just plagiarize somebody else's idea and make it our own."

"I don't want to do a camp either. I was thinking we could come up with something unique. The camp really helped the younger kids, but we both know that it's the older kids in foster care who really need the help."

Celeste glared at her. "You mean kids like me? The ones that nobody ever wanted? The ones who age out of the system because they're so unlovable?"

Abigail felt bad for Celeste. What must she think of herself to say things like that?

"I don't think you were unlovable, Celeste. I think you were damaged, and you acted out in a way that pushed people away from you."

"Are you blaming me for never getting adopted?"

"Of course not! I can't win with you. I'm trying to be supportive."

"Well, I don't need your support!" she said, standing up and walking over to the refrigerator. She pulled out the ground beef and then retrieved a frying pan from the cabinet.

"I know you don't need anything from me, but right now, we need each other. We have to come up with something. And the sooner that we do it and make it successful, the sooner we can sell this place, cash our checks and go our separate ways forever. Isn't that what you want?"

"Absolutely," Celeste said, opening the package and dumping the big brick of meat into the frying pan.

"Then we need to come up with something. Maybe we should go meet with my new friend and see if she has some ideas. She's got contacts with the foster care system because she adopted a little boy that went to her camp."

"Fine. See if she has any ideas."

"She gave me her number, so I will text her after dinner. Look, Celeste, I know this isn't easy for either of us. But if we're going to make this work, you've got to stop fighting me all the time. Can't we just call a truce for the next three months?"

Celeste turned the heat on and used a large plastic spoon to break up the meat in the pan. "Fine. I will do my best to play nicely if you will do your best not to annoy me."

Abigail rolled her eyes and walked out of

the room, realizing that Celeste was doing the best that she could. She would take what she could get at this point.

* * *

BEING LATE AUGUST, Dylan was getting ready to start school again in a few days. Dawson and Julie had taken him over to the bakery to get a treat as the last moments of summer wound down.

"I want the chocolate pound cake, but I also want some of those snickerdoodle cookies!" Dylan said, grinning happily as he directed his grandmother on what he wanted.

"Now, Dylan, you know you can't have that much sugar!" Julie said, squeezing his shoulders from behind.

"Oh, Julie, leave the boy alone. Kids need sugar," SuAnn said, waving her hand.

Julie put her hands on her hips. "Excuse me, but are you the same woman who made me finish a plate full of vegetables before I could even take a bite of my own birthday cake?"

"Well, that was then, and this is now. And if my Dylan wants dessert, that's what my Dylan is going to get! Come on behind the counter with me so we can get out of earshot of the food police over there," she said, pulling on Dylan's little hand.

He happily ran around the counter as the two of them disappeared into the back, probably to fill Dylan's gullet with a bag full of sugar.

"Can you believe her?" Julie asked, looking up at Dawson. He stood there, a smile on his face. "What's so funny?"

"I just like to see you and your mother spar. It's entertaining."

Julie chuckled. "It's not at all entertaining for me. That kid is going to have diabetes before he even goes to his first class."

"Don't worry. I ate tons of sugar as a kid, and I'm healthy as a horse."

Julie looked down at her phone and sent a quick text. "I'm inviting Abigail and Celeste over for dinner tonight. They need someone to help them brainstorm ideas for what to do with Elaine Benson's house."

"Oh, good. I'm looking forward to meeting them."

"Abigail is lovely. But I've heard that Celeste is extremely difficult. She had a rough past and ended up in foster care until she aged out. And she is still holding a grudge against Elaine for some reason. And Abigail."

"That ought to be an interesting dinner then."

"Yeah, I'm afraid so. I was thinking of making meatloaf. Do you think that's okay?"

"Of course, as long as we make Lucy's gravy to go with the mashed potatoes."

Julie held up her phone. "No problem. Lucy left me all of our favorite recipes."

Dylan came running back out of the storage room, a bag full of goodies in his hand. "Grandma gave me cookies and pound cake and also these little donuts and…"

SuAnn slipped her hand over his mouth. "We don't tell all of our secrets, Dylan."

"Grandma wants to know if I can eat dinner at her house tonight," Dylan said, holding his hands in a prayer position and squeezing his adorable face.

"Actually, that's great timing because we're having dinner guests over tonight."

"Your dinner guests are always boring!"

Julie pinched the end of his nose. "Then I guess it's a good thing you're going to your grandma's."

"Why don't you just let him sleep over?"

"Fine, but just know when he eats all that sugar, you're not to call me to come pick him up."

SuAnn laughed and rolled her eyes. "He's not the first grandchild I've ever had. I remember when Meg spent the night one time and ate so much candy that she threw up all over my favorite living room rug."

Julie shook her head, laughing. Her phone suddenly started vibrating in her pocket and she pulled it out to see that it was Colleen wanting to do a video chat. She was desperately missing her daughters, so this was a welcome opportunity to check in with them.

"Colleen!" Julie said, so happy to see her face. Dawson stood behind her, waving. SuAnn and Dylan joined in as well.

"Oh, wow, everybody's there. Where is Aunt Janine?"

"She went to try on dresses again today."

"Without you?"

"I think she needed some time alone. She's having a little difficulty figuring out what kind of wedding she wants. You know how the women in this family can be indecisive," she said, giggling.

Colleen smiled broadly. "I was kind of hoping she was there, but that's okay. I'll catch up with her later."

"Where is Meg?"

"She took Vivi down to the river. I think they're looking for turtles or something."

"I sure miss my granddaughter. When are y'all coming back?"

"I think in another couple of weeks. We had some more places we wanted to see, but

Tucker really needs to get back. He has some business meetings coming up before the holiday season."

"Well, I can't wait to see all of you in person and give you big hugs. You can't leave for this long again!"

"It's so good to see your face, dear," SuAnn said, blowing a kiss at her granddaughter.

"Good to see you too, Grandma. Are you starting school soon, Dylan?"

"Yeah, in a few days. But I get to spend the night with Grandma tonight!"

"That's awesome, buddy! Have fun."

"You look like you're having a wonderful time, Colleen," Dawson said, putting his hands on Julie's shoulders and leaning down toward the phone.

"More than I can even describe," she said, grinning from ear to ear.

"What's going on with you?" Julie asked.

"Well, I was going to wait until we were all together again, but I just can't hold it in."

She turned around and waved, and then Tucker appeared beside her.

"Wait for what?"

To Julie's surprise, Colleen held up her left hand and there was a ring that hadn't been there before. It was a beautiful engagement ring with a round stone.

"We're engaged!" they both shouted at the same time.

Julie squealed. "Congratulations! Tucker finally gets to join our crazy family!"

"I can't wait," he said, laughing.

"I am so excited for you both. Everybody's getting married!"

"Yes, I guess we're all going to be a bunch of old married women before too long. But that's okay because I get to marry my very best friend," she said, looking at him with adoration.

"Congratulations, y'all, really. That's awesome!" Dawson said.

SuAnn congratulated them, and Dylan wandered off somewhere else in the store

because what little kid cared about en-
gagements?

"I better go. We're having an engagement
dinner out tonight, so I need to go find Meg.
I'll tell you all about the romantic proposal
when I get home."

Julie could feel her eyes welling with
tears. Her daughters were grown up now. As
much as she loved being a grandmother, she
longed for those days when they were just
little girls, completely dependent on her,
playing dress up and dreaming of being
princesses.

"Congratulations again to you both, and
we love you very much."

"We love you too," Colleen said, smiling
and waving before she ended the call.

CHAPTER 8

*B*en walked around the square, this time being very careful not to knock somebody over. He was normally a pretty even keeled individual, but uprooting his life and coming back to Seagrove after so many years had really thrown him for a loop.

It wasn't like he didn't have a choice. He could've gone anywhere in the world, but he chose to come back here. Part of it was because he and Dawson had had such a great friendship all those years ago. The other part of it was that Seagrove had been the only place he'd ever lived that actually felt like home.

Now, however, he was wondering if he had made the wrong decision. It seemed like every commercial space in town was rented, and he had no clue where he was going to put his office. The whole idea behind coming back was to open a small town pediatric practice where he could really get to know his patients.

Having worked in the big city for so many years, he was looking forward to a slower pace. It would mean less money, of course, but that's not why he had become a doctor. He truly wanted to help people, and part of that was because of his little sister. He didn't like to think about that, though.

He'd been walking around for days, trying to find any little out-of-the-way office space that might work. Everywhere was either already rented out long term, or it was way too small to be a doctor's office.

Finally, he'd spotted one place that looked like it was empty. It was off the square, down a side road, but he thought he could make it work. He had called the owner to have him open it up and see if the space might be adequate.

"You Ben Callaway?"

A gruff old man, grizzled one might call him, opened the front door of the small brick home, which was zoned commercial. From the outside, it looked like it might have been workable, even though he would have to really promote the office because no one would find it so far outside of the commercial part of town.

"That's me. I appreciate you letting me see the place today."

The man, not cracking a smile, opened the door and stepped back. "Well, what're you waiting for? Come on."

Ben walked through the door and was immediately assaulted by the smell of mold and mildew. The place was a wreck. It looked like no upkeep had ever been done since it was built, probably back in the fifties.

"Wow. I didn't realize it needed so many repairs."

The man closed the door loudly behind them and stared at him, a scowl on his face. "You always walk into somebody's house and badmouth it?"

"Oh, no, sir. I didn't mean to offend..."

"You said you needed an office, and this is an office. What are you complaining about?"

Ben was suddenly worried he was about to be kidnapped or murdered. This guy seemed to have a serious ax to grind. Maybe he had watched one too many true crime shows on TV.

"No offense, really. I was just looking for something that was a little more... move in ready."

"Oh, this place just needs some sweeping out. Maybe some paint."

Ben looked around, being careful to stay near the front door in case he had to make a run for it. There were cobwebs hanging from pretty much every corner of the room. The hardwood floor had holes in it, and he was too scared to walk any further into the house.

The smell was a mixture of the aforementioned mold and mildew mixed with a little bit of dead animal. He assumed there were quite a few underneath the house. And he could hear the wind blowing outside even though the door was closed. As he peeked around the corner into the kitchen, he realized there was a big hole in the back wall.

"You have a huge hole back there."

"Oh, nothing that a little of spackle won't fix," the man said, swiping his hand in the air. The hole was at least as big as a basketball, certainly not something spackle was going to repair.

"Look, Mr. Abernathy, I appreciate you meeting me out here on such short notice. However, I don't think this place is going to suit my needs."

"Well, this was a waste of time," he said under his breath. "I have things to do." Without saying another word, the man turned around and walked to the back of the house, a door slamming in the distance. Assuming their meeting was over, Ben made a hasty retreat out of the house and down the sidewalk.

* * *

JANINE STOOD in front of the mirror at the dress store. She had never been so sick of trying on dresses in all her life. If she only needed one reason to never get divorced, it was just so she didn't have to ever get married again and pick out a wedding dress.

She had already been through this process a couple of times with her sister in tow, but this time she just wanted to do it on her own. She wanted to see if she connected with any of the dresses without someone else's input.

Maybe it was her age or her experience, but this whole wedding planning thing was a lot more stress than she had expected. She just wanted to get married. She just wanted to call William her husband and hear him call her his wife.

In reality, that little piece of paper that they would be given at the courthouse meant little to her. She was already planning to spend the rest of her life with William, whether they ever got married.

"What did you think about that last one?" the woman at the dress shop near Charleston asked her. Poor lady was probably exhausted. She'd been running her ragged all day long trying to find the perfect dress. Every single one of them was either too white or too cream, too long or too short, too poofy or too plain.

"I don't know. There's just something about it that doesn't suit me. I think it was a little too much. Too fancy. Too much lace."

She could tell the lady was struggling really hard not to just roll her eyes and quit her job right there on the spot. But she was doing well to coddle Janine just enough that she didn't break down in tears right there in the middle of the store.

"I understand. I have one more I want to show you. I think we might have been going about this all wrong. We just got a new product line in yesterday, so let me go grab one in your size."

Janine didn't hold out much hope. At this point, she was thinking that wearing her blue jeans and a T-shirt might be the best option. All she cared about was that at the end of her wedding day, she had a ring on her finger and a new last name.

"Here it is. Why don't you go give this one a try?" The woman smiled, although it was plastered on like she was forcing it. Possibly fake. This woman just wanted to get her to the checkout, ring her up and send her on her way. And Janine couldn't blame her.

She went into the dressing room, slipped off the dress she was currently wearing, and unzipped the garment bag the woman had handed her. Almost as soon as she unzipped it, a feeling came over her. And when she saw the dress, she realized it was *the one*.

It had beautiful beading in all the right

places, a minimal amount of sequins woven into the beaded areas, and it was just the right length. The perfect shape. This was her dress!

She quickly slipped it on, and it fit like a glove. Honestly, it was like she could hear the angels singing and the clouds were finally parting. This was the dress that she was going to wear at her wedding. She couldn't believe it. She had to stop herself for just a moment before she went out to stand in front of the mirrors for fear that she might run across the store and kiss that saleswoman right on the lips. Maybe things were finally looking up.

CELESTE SAT in the rocking chair on the back deck, watching the last remnants of daylight streak across the sky. Although they didn't get perfect sunset view over the ocean, it was enough to see the little wisps of pink and orange.

Thankfully, Abigail had disappeared somewhere inside the house, doing a conference call for her work. She was a lot more able to work virtually than Celeste was. It wasn't like she could develop a neighborhood from several states away.

Her hands rested atop yet another one of Elaine's journals. She had browsed through some of them, finding a lot of it quite boring. But this one, when she had opened it earlier this morning, had Celeste's name in it several times.

She honestly didn't know why she kept reading these journals. It wasn't like it was going to change anything. It wouldn't change how she felt about Elaine, or how Elaine had felt about her. Elaine Benson was dead. It wasn't like they could have conversations or work things out.

Still, her curiosity was just getting the best of her. She had always been that kind of person, the one who wanted to know the latest gossip or ask a million questions.

She opened up the journal and immediately noticed that the first entry had her name.

Celeste has been getting in trouble at school. She cheated on a test, slapped another girl on the arm and even got caught smoking behind the concession stand at the football stadium. I don't know what I'm going to do with her. The social worker said that it's best if she goes to a group home, but I don't want that for her.

I keep trying and trying to get through to her. But every time I speak, she snaps at me. It's like trying to pet a dog that's been whipped by some terrible, angry human being.

I just don't know what to do.

Celeste shut the book and stared out over the water again, closing her eyes and taking a breath. She didn't know why these journals were getting to her. It wasn't like she was an emotional person, but there was a part of her that felt sorry for her younger self.

She knew she didn't deserve the kind of childhood she had, and there were moments she wished things could've been different. She wished she had been raised by her birth mother, and that she'd had the childhood other people got to have. The one where there's a mom and a dad, family vacations, a great big golden retriever in all the Christmas photos. She wished she could've had a room mother who brought cupcakes and went on field trips and served on the PTA.

Instead, she had abandonment, a series of terrible foster homes, a group home and then that wonderful moment where she was thrown out into the world and told good luck.

She opened the journal again, telling herself this would be the last time. It didn't matter what else it said. It was all water under the bridge, ancient history. And history couldn't be undone.

Today, I saw Celeste sitting underneath the willow tree. She didn't know I could see her. She was crying. Everything in me wanted to go out and give her a hug, pull her close to me like a good mother would.

I spoke to the social worker today about the

possibility of adopting Celeste. They advised against it, told me she had so many issues that it wouldn't be advisable. And then they told me that if I adopted her, I could never foster another child because they wouldn't trust having her in the home. They said she needs to move now since I have little ones here. It's so hard to make this decision. She seems to hate it here, so am I doing her any favors adopting her? And what about all the kids in this state who are going to need me?

This is an impossible situation.

Celeste was stunned. Elaine had considered adopting her? That was completely new information that she hadn't expected to read. She felt a stray tear roll down her cheek. Angry that she was getting so emotional, she slammed the journal shut.

"Are you okay?"

Abigail, like some kind of stealth eavesdropper, walked up behind her.

"You scared me to death. What do you want?" she said without turning around.

"It's time for us to head to dinner at Julie's house. Remember?"

No, she hadn't remembered. And she really didn't feel like going to meet new people, but Abigail was insistent that Julie could help them figure out how to use the house. And they needed all the help they could get. Plus, she was starving.

"I'll be inside in a minute."

Abigail lingered for a few more seconds before going back into the house and shutting the door. Celeste didn't know what to do with what she had just read, but it didn't matter now. Elaine hadn't adopted her, and Elaine wasn't her mother. Why did she feel like she'd just lost something?

THERE WAS nothing worse than meeting new people. Celeste had always hated it. Maybe it was because she was so tall and always towered over everyone, making her stand out. Maybe it was because she had some level of social anxiety and always feared she was saying the wrong thing. She found it ironic that everyone seemed to fear her, yet the reason she was so abrasive was because she feared everyone else.

Abigail rang the doorbell and took a couple of steps back. Everyone liked Abigail. She was neutral. Easy to talk to. Not confrontational. Normal sized.

"Hey, Abigail! So good to see you again," the woman said before looking at Celeste. "I'm Julie. It's nice to finally meet you, Celeste." She opened the door further to allow them in. Why did Julie have to be so darn short and cute? It just made Celeste feel taller than she was.

"Thanks for having us," Celeste said, trying to sound friendly and chipper, but it came out sounding more like she was a pubescent boy whose voice was in the middle of changing.

"Your house is beautiful, Julie. I love that china cabinet," Abigail said, looking around the room.

"Thank you. This is Dawson's family

home, and that was his grandmother's china cabinet."

"Did somebody call my name?"

A very handsome guy appeared from another room, a smile on his face. He looked like an out-of-place cowboy with his masculine physique and purposely messed-up hairstyle. He was a mixture of ranch hand and surfer dude.

"I was just telling Abigail and Celeste how this was your grandmother's home."

"I'm Dawson. Nice to meet you both," he said, his southern drawl right out of a textbook.

"Nice to meet you. I've heard wonderful things about you," Abigail said. Celeste just forced a smile and tried to act like a normal human being. Social interactions had always been harder for her, but she figured it was because she'd had no loving parents to show her how to act in the world. Sometimes, she said the wrong thing and offended people even when she wasn't intending to do that. Other times, she just had the filter between her mouth and brain turned to the off position, and things came out that shouldn't have.

"Why don't we go ahead into the dining room, and we can chat in there? I hope y'all like meatloaf?"

Celeste really didn't like meatloaf all that much, but she was willing to try it again. Maybe Julie knew how to make it a different way than what she'd had previously. Throughout her years in foster care, she'd had the cooking of many different "moms". Elaine had actually been a pretty good cook, but the rest of them bordered on giving her food poisoning.

They walked into the dining room, and the table was already set. Everything was fancier than Celeste had envisioned, especially being in a small Southern town. But things at Julie's house were very proper, probably because the house had belonged to Dawson's grandmother.

"You can have a seat anywhere," she said, smiling as she took her seat, and Dawson sat down beside her. "We will have another guest joining us soon. Dawson has a friend staying with us right now."

"Great, I'm always interested in meeting new people," Abigail said, smiling. Celeste couldn't tell if she actually meant that, or she was just making polite conversation.

"So, I understand that you ladies have to come up with a use for Elaine Benson's house?" Dawson said, before taking a sip of his tea.

"Yes, and it's proving to be a bit challenging. We're not sure what to do with it."

"Abigail and I are very different people, so I think we have conflicting ideas on the best course of action."

"I know that foster care is very close to Abigail's heart. Do you feel the same way, Celeste?" Julie asked as she passed the plate of biscuits toward Celeste.

"I mean, I think foster care is obviously important and needs to be completely overhauled. I'm just not sure what we can do about that."

"Celeste isn't interested in having a camp or working with little kids," Abigail said, not making eye contact with her. She plopped a glob of mashed potatoes on her plate and focused on them instead.

"You know, I think it's the older kids who really need the help anyway," Dawson said. "When we ran the camp, I spoke to some of the social workers who came by, and they wished they had something to help their older kids who were about to age out."

"I aged out, and I can tell you I got little in the way of education about going out into the world as an eighteen-year-old kid. It was hard."

"Maybe that's where to focus?" Julie said.

"But how? We can't foster them if they're aging out," Abigail said.

Just as Celeste was about to give her input, the door swung open. "Sorry I'm late. I had a hysterical new mother on the phone. Kid with colic." She looked up to see the guy who'd knocked her over standing beside her. "Celeste?"

"Wait. You two know each other?" Dawson asked, staring at each of them.

Ben laughed. "Kind of. Remember, I told you I knocked a woman down on the sidewalk?"

Celeste held up her elbow to showcase the bandage that was still there.

"Oh, my gosh! Are you okay?" Celeste nodded, stifling a laugh. "Ben, you're a big oaf!"

"I know, I know. I apologized already. Even offered her twenty bucks for pain and suffering, but she wouldn't take it," he said to Dawson as he sat down across from her and put his napkin in his lap.

"Twenty bucks?"

"It's all the cash I had on me at the time," he said, pouring a glass of sweet tea.

"Sorry my old friend almost killed you," Dawson said, winking at her. "He's like one of those large dogs that doesn't know his own strength."

Ben rolled his eyes. "You're over-exaggerating. But I am sorry, Celeste. Truly."

She smiled. It was a real, genuine smile. She hadn't felt one of those in a long time.

"No problem. Just don't get distracted by any more dogs or you could kill someone."

Ben let out a loud laugh. "You're funny. So, what did I miss?"

"Celeste and Abigail were foster children at Elaine Benson's house when they were kids. Elaine recently passed, and she left the house to them. To fully earn it, they have to do something good with it for the next three months before they can sell it. We're trying to help them come up with a good idea," Julie said, quickly filling him in.

"Got it. Wow, that's a crazy idea Elaine Benson had. Have you come up with anything?"

"We were talking about older foster kids, the ones who are about to age out. We thought maybe they could do something like that. Celeste aged out."

He looked at her. "I know that had to be tough." His voice was softer now, but he didn't look like he pitied her. He just looked kind.

"It was. When a kid ages out, most of them are unemployed or at least under-employed. They've had little to no financial training, so they don't know how to budget, get an apartment or even open a bank account. Many of the girls end up pregnant very quickly."

"I've seen many foster kids in my years as a doctor..."

"You're a doctor?" Celeste asked, shocked.

"Ben is a pediatrician," Dawson said.

"I used to be. Now I can't find office space in Seagrove, so maybe I'll work at the ice cream shop or mow the grass for old people."

"So you moved back to Seagrove recently?" Abigail asked.

"A few days ago. I guess I thought finding commercial space would be easy, but it's impossible so far. Businesses here tend to stay around for decades."

"What brought you back here?" Celeste

asked, finally trying a bite of her meatloaf. It was actually very good.

"A divorce, mainly. I was looking to relive some good old days with my buddy here, too," he said, smiling as he looked at Dawson. Celeste wondered what it was like to have roots. To have friends. To have deep feelings like that.

"Sorry to hear about the divorce," Celeste said, feeling awkward.

"It's okay. Sometimes things aren't meant to be. Anyway, let's get back to the whole house thing. I'm very intrigued about what you ladies are going to do."

Abigail laughed. "Yeah, we're intrigued too."

CHAPTER 9

*A*fter dinner, they all retired to the deck beside the inn. Overlooking the ocean, the deck was lit with string lights and a few tiki torches. Abigail could hear the rolling waves in the distance as they crashed against the shoreline. There was nothing better than the sound of the ocean.

Celeste and Ben seemed to be hitting it off, and she was shocked. She'd never seen Celeste interacting with other humans in such a... well, human way. She seemed at ease, almost relaxed, as they chatted about this and that. Throughout dinner, Abigail struggled not to stare, and she truly wanted to ask Ben what his secret was. How did he make Celeste nice?

"So you mentioned you live in Texas, right?" Ben asked as they sat around a small fire pit.

"Yeah. I manage the development of sub-divisions, mostly." She looked down at her bowl of peach cobbler.

"That's amazing. I imagine you have a lot of construction skills then?"

"I do. I can renovate or build just about anything." Celeste definitely wasn't lacking in confidence, Abigail thought to herself. That was one area where she herself was lacking. Abigail had struggled with self-confidence for much of her life.

"What about you, Abigail? Do you work?"

"I was working in public relations back in Nashville, and I'm still doing some remote work."

"Do you like it?"

She shrugged her shoulders. "It pays the bills."

She wished she had a career she loved, but so far, it hadn't happened. She didn't know what she really wanted to do with her life.

"You know, I had a crazy thought while we were talking over dinner," Julie said.

"What's that?"

"Well, Elaine's house is pretty large, and Ben needs a space for his practice."

"And?" Dawson said, laughing.

"That huge front room could work."

"You mean the formal living room and dining room combo?" Abigail asked.

"Yes. Elaine never used it much, did she? That's what Dixie said, anyway."

"We're just using it for storage," Celeste said. "I mean, as we pull things from the other rooms and the attic, we're storing them there before taking them to the thrift store or the dump."

"I wouldn't want to intrude. Besides, Celeste doesn't sound like she's a big fan of little kids," he said, chuckling.

"Actually, I'm not a big fan of little kids

that I personally have to take care of, but you would take care of them so that would be fine by me."

"What if we end up selling in three months? Ben will not want to move his practice."

"It might just buy me some time until I can find a commercial space. Or maybe I might buy the old Benson house from you," he said, mulling over ideas.

"Why don't you come take a look tomorrow? See if it will even work?" Celeste offered. Abigail had never seen this laid-back side of her, and it was a little foreign to her. Still, anytime Celeste wasn't biting her head off was a good time.

Ben nodded and smiled. "That sounds like a good idea. Are you okay with this, Abigail?"

"Of course. I think it would be great for Seagrove to have a new pediatrician. But I don't think it's going to satisfy the three women who have to judge us."

"I think you two need to go sit down with

my contact over at social services. I feel strongly that she is going to have some ideas for you."

Abigail agreed. "I'll send her a text right now. Maybe we can get together sometime tomorrow too."

* * *

"I LIKE THIS ONE," William said, setting his fork down on the edge of the plate.

Janine looked at him, frustrated. "That's the very first one. We have six more to try."

As they sat in the small back room of the bakery, she looked at the miniature sample cakes in front of them. Her mother didn't make wedding cakes, so they were at a bakery closer to Charleston that specialized in them. Laid out before them were chocolate, vanilla, lemon, raspberry... She could barely keep up with all the options.

"What's so wrong with me liking that one?"

"Don't you want to have the perfect wedding cake?"

William laughed. "Cake is cake, honey. I like all cakes. Chocolate, vanilla, red velvet… Heck, if you mixed up a bowl of flour and sugar, I'd probably eat it with a spoon."

"You try the rest of these before you make a choice. Have a drink of water. It'll cleanse your pallet."

William sighed and slid the next cake closer to him. "You know I don't care about things like this."

"I know you don't," she said. "But it's the only wedding we'll ever have, and we might as well have the best cake possible."

"Fine. I'll try the rest of these cakes as long as you promise I don't have to go to that meeting at the florist about the flowers."

She scrunched her face up in annoyance. "But that's tomorrow. You promised you would go."

He turned in his chair to face her. "Janine, I'm a man. We don't give one hoot about flowers. Please, for the love of all that is good and holy, don't make me go to the flower meeting. I will feel my manhood slipping away moment by moment, petal by petal."

Janine couldn't help but laugh. "Okay, but you have to try each one of these cakes and actually tell me what you think. I want this to be right."

He smiled. "You have yourself a deal."

* * *

CELESTE AND ABIGAIL sat in the small waiting room at the social services office. It was about thirty minutes from Seagrove, and they had ridden together, mostly in silence. Celeste was trying as best as she could to keep the peace with Abigail. Still, they'd argued about the radio station, what their middle school mascot was - Celeste won since she knew it was an eagle - and they'd even fought about what to put the thermostat on at night.

"Ladies, you can come on back," the receptionist said, waving at them from the doorway. They followed her down the hall to a conference room. It reminded Celeste a lot of the closing tables she sat at during her time in real estate.

"I really hope she can give us some useful information," Abigail said, finally breaking their silence.

"Me too."

Thankfully, the woman entered the room pretty quickly after that, which alleviated the need for more boring small talk.

"Sorry to keep you waiting. We had some issues with a foster situation this morning that required my attention." Julie had given them the name of Cassandra Dalton, although she wasn't the person they had worked with at the camp. That woman was apparently out on vacation.

"No problem. I was enjoying looking at your binders out there. Lots of adoption success stories." Abigail always knew just the right thing to say, and that was quite annoying to Celeste.

"Yes, I am very blessed to get to do what I

do for a living, although some days it just breaks your heart."

"I can imagine."

"So what can I do for you?"

"We have a house over in Seagrove. We need to make use of it, and we were hoping you could give us some ideas," Celeste blurted out.

"You want ideas for your house? Like decorating ideas?" Cassandra asked, tilting her head like she didn't understand what in the world Celeste was talking about.

"It's kind of a weird situation. We were both foster children decades ago and one of our foster mothers left us a house together. The stipulation is that we can't take full ownership of the home until we complete a task. For the next three months, we are to work together on a good cause while using the house. Something that will benefit the community."

Her mouth dropped open slightly. "Wow. That's a really unique proposition. So you're looking to take in some foster children?"

Celeste let out a very loud, inappropriate laugh. "Absolutely not. We're not looking to create a family here. We just want to do a good thing so we can sell the house in three months."

Now she'd done it. She should've just let Abigail continue taking care of the conversation. Instead, she had probably offended the woman.

"I see. So you're not looking to become foster parents?"

"No. While that's a wonderful thing, it's just not right for the situation," Abigail said, smiling sweetly. She could really turn it on when she needed to. "I think what we're looking for is some guidance on how we might be able to best help those who are going to age out of the system. Celeste had that experience, and from what she's explained, it wasn't a good one."

Cassandra looked at her, and it made her feel like she was under a microscope suddenly. "You aged out? That's a really tough situation."

She didn't like to feel that she was being pitied, so she squared her shoulders, set her jaw and forced a slight smile. "It was hard, but you learn to toughen up when you've lived the life I have."

"Celeste was left at a fire station when she was just three years old," Abigail said, her voice dripping in pity. Celeste could feel anger welling up inside of her, and she used all of her strength to push it back down.

"This really isn't about me, Abigail," she said, glaring at her. She could immediately tell that Abigail got the message as she cleared her throat and looked back at Cassandra.

"Well, I'm very sorry you had those experiences, but you're both right. It's our older foster youth who are about to age out of the system that really need the most help. They get thrown into a world they don't understand, most of them unemployed and uneducated."

"We're hoping that you can help us think of ways to use the house, even if only temporarily, to help that part of the foster system," Abigail said.

Cassandra thought for a few moments. "What about some kind of educational program?"

"Educational program? You mean like teaching school?" Celeste asked.

"No. I'm thinking about something more like life education. Where they could come every day and learn a new life skill. Cooking, budgeting, doing a résumé, that sort of thing."

Celeste had to admit that it was a good idea. It would probably be sufficient to meet Elaine's stipulation of them doing something good with the home, and it would be beneficial to the kids. Plus, she would've benefitted from something like that when she aged out.

"How many kids do you think you would have who need this?"

"Oh, at least ten. We could pull them from the surrounding areas. It would be a very useful program. You know twenty-five percent of foster children who age out of the system end up with PTSD from all the unstable relationships and abuse. We might even have a counselor come in to help them with that."

"I think this could be a fantastic idea," Abigail said. "Is it something that we could get started pretty quickly?"

Cassandra smiled. "Well, that depends. Are you two equipped to teach them things like cooking and budgeting?"

Abigail looked at Celeste. "I think so. Celeste is a wonderful cook, and I can do a mean résumé. We can also come up with some other things to teach them. We have a few friends in Seagrove who might even help us."

"Wonderful! Then I will start the paperwork. If you can come up with a list of what you want to offer in your education program, I will create some materials to send out to our satellite offices. I would think that we could get started fairly quickly."

"I can't believe we're really doing this,"

Celeste said, feeling more nervous than she'd expected.

Cassandra put her hands on the table. "The need is great. We have several girls who are really struggling right now, and they are aging out very soon. What you're doing could change the course of their lives."

As Cassandra stood up and walked toward the door, Celeste felt the weight of the responsibility on her shoulders. She knew exactly what it was like to be sent out into the world with no help. For the first time in her life, she felt like she was about to do something important, and she would not let those kids down.

* * *

BEN STOOD on the front porch after knocking on the door. He had so enjoyed his dinner with Julie, Dawson, Abigail and Celeste the night before. In fact, he was liking his interactions with Celeste more and more.

She was tough, that was for sure. She

was a strong, independent woman, and she was a little scary at times. Julie had talked to him after Celeste and Abigail left and told him about the checkered history between the two women. Abigail was nice and cordial, but Celeste was interesting.

He saw something in her. An inner strength that most people didn't have. An edge that made her intriguing.

The door swung open, and Celeste stood there, wearing a pair of jeans, a gray T-shirt and a pair of sneakers. She was tall and thin, but athletic. She wore no makeup except for what appeared to be some tinted lip balm, and her hair was long and straight, cascading down her back and ending about halfway down.

"Hey. Come on in."

Ben walked inside and looked around. He had never been in Elaine's house before, although he had seen it from the outside a million times. The willow tree out front was very well known, and people often stopped to take a picture in front of it. It was huge, after all.

The house sat right on the ocean with one of the most beautiful views in the entire area. Being a big Victorian home, it brought the feeling of history to Seagrove.

"Wow. This place is beautiful."

Celeste shrugged her shoulders. "I suppose so if you like that kind of thing. I'm not much into the older style houses myself."

"Oh, that's right. You work in new construction, right?"

"That's what I've been doing for the last few years. I actually prefer working with my hands and building stuff, but managing the developments made me a lot more money."

"Do you plan to go back to that when you leave Seagrove?"

"I'm not sure. If I end up selling this place, I'll make a lot of money. That might give me the option to try something new."

"What would you like to try?"

She laughed. "I have no idea. I've never been given the chance to think about something like that. When you're a foster kid, you learn that dreaming is a dangerous thing."

Hearing her say that made him feel sad. Of course, over the years, he'd often heard about foster kids who had aged out of the system, but he had never treated one of those people. Being a pediatrician, most of his kids were on the younger side, so by the time someone hit eighteen years old they were typically seeing a regular general practitioner.

He could obviously see what it had done to Celeste. Being in foster care her entire life and then being thrown out into the world had hardened her, made her not trust people. It had probably even stunted some of her social skills, which was why she was having such a hard time with Abigail.

"So this is the area you were thinking for my office?"

She nodded. After walking in the front door, the room immediately on the left-hand side was a formal living room. There were two French doors leading into the room, which would give great privacy for his office. He could easily put some drapes on the doors to make it a completely separate space.

She opened one of the doors, and they walked into the room. It was rather large and had an adjoining formal dining room that looked like it hadn't been used in many years.

"I have no idea what kind of space you need for an office, but since you said there are no commercial pieces of real estate available right now, maybe this would be workable."

He walked around both rooms, trying to assess the size, and how he would set things up.

"I think we could have the reception desk right up here and put a few chairs along each wall for the waiting area. We could have a room divider and then a small triage area set up over here..." he said as he moved around each room.

"Sounds like it could work."

"And over here in the dining room, I really only need one examining room because I'm only one doctor. My nurse could handle everything else out in the triage area." He turned around and smiled. "I honestly think it could work out really well."

"That's great. I'm not sure about the zoning, though."

"Well, Dawson said he has connections over at the zoning office, of course," he said, laughing.

"I'm pretty sure Dawson has connections everywhere."

"I guess it's one of the perks of having him as a friend. Anyway, he thinks he can get me a special permit to do this, as long as you and Abigail agree."

She chuckled under her breath. "Getting me and Abigail to agree about anything is a little difficult, but I think she'll be okay with it. After all, we're probably going to be busy with our new project."

He sat down on one of the storage totes. Celeste sat down across from him on a wooden crate.

"So you had your meeting with the woman at foster care?"

"Yeah, and she gave us some good ideas. I'm not quite sure how all of it's going to be put together just yet, but our focus will be on girls who are about to age out of the foster care system, probably between the ages of sixteen and eighteen. We'll be teaching them about things like how to make a résumé, cooking, budgeting, and any other topics we think they will need to know when they go out into the world."

"I think that's amazing, Celeste," he said with a smile. There was just something about her and the way that she was so gruff on the outside to so many people, but they were able to immediately connect.

Having just come out of a divorce, Ben hadn't been thinking about dating at all. His marriage had been on the rocks for a long time, and he had forgotten what it was like to be able to sit down and have a pleasant conversation with a woman. Most of the conversations he'd had with his wife in recent years had turned into arguments or not speaking for days on end.

"Hopefully it will be a good thing, and it will be sufficient for us to be able to sell the home in three months."

"So you're sure you want to sell it? Do you want to leave Seagrove?"

"I never wanted to come back here. It wasn't on my bucket list by any means."

"But you lived here as a kid, right?"

"Just for a couple of years when I was around fourteen."

"How did you and Elaine Benson get along?"

"You know, I was a wild child. I'll admit that I was really hard to handle. But I always got the feeling that she didn't like me at all and she adored Abigail. In fact, Abigail was always her golden child. They kept a relationship going for decades, but I never saw her or spoke to her again after I left."

He didn't know what to make of what she'd just said. From all accounts, Elaine Benson had been a lovely woman who adored children and did everything she could to help them. He found it hard to believe that she wouldn't like Celeste that much.

"Well, I'd better get back. I promised Dawson that I would help him with a couple of chores at the inn. Making me earn my keep, I guess," he said, laughing as he stood up.

"Hopefully Dawson can get the zoning worked out, and then you're free to move in here as soon as you want."

"Thanks, Celeste. If you hadn't suggested this, I'd still be wandering around downtown knocking people over and staring at dogs."

Without warning, she let out a huge laugh, something he hadn't expected. It was nice.

"Sorry," she said, putting her hand over her mouth. "I'm a big woman, which leads to a very big laugh."

"I like it," he said, unable to keep himself from smiling. There was a long, awkward silence before she cleared her throat.

"I'd better get to work. There are some things I need to rearrange for us to start working with the foster kids."

"Right. Don't want to interfere with that. I'll touch base with you soon about the office."

She walked him to the door and opened it, waving at him as he descended the stairs. When he turned around again, she had already closed the door and disappeared inside.

CHAPTER 10

*I*t had been three weeks since Celeste and Abigail had met with Cassandra, but they were finally cleared to work with some of the foster kids. It had taken that long to get the house set up to have the space to teach them what they needed to know.

Abigail was really excited, partially because she was ready to do something good in the world but also because it was getting harder and harder to just live in the house alone with Celeste.

Mostly, they stayed out of each other's way. But there were moments where they butted heads over everything from Abigail leaving her shoes by the front door to playing her music too loud in the mornings while Celeste was still trying to sleep. It was a big house, but they seemed to be able to find ways to annoy each other, nonetheless.

Of course, the foster kids would not be living with them, but they would be at the house at least five days a week for most of the day. Abigail had gathered up all kinds of business people from the local community to come and help teach the kids for free.

She had an accountant doing a whole series of classes about budgeting, balancing checkbooks and other important financial considerations.

She had a personal chef coming to teach them how to cook, grocery shop, and manage a household.

She had a real estate agent coming to explain how to improve their credit, rent an apartment, or even buy a house at some point.

She had a human resources professional coming to explain how to create a résumé, look for jobs, and build a career.

She and Celeste would also help with all of those topics, giving their input and working one on one with any kids who needed it. Mainly, they would manage the entire project.

It was a little daunting to think about working so closely with Celeste every day, but it was a means to an end. If the two of them could just play nice long enough, the three months would be over. After all, they only had about two months left, anyway.

Dawson had managed to get a special zoning permit for Ben to use the two front rooms as his office. He had already started moving things in, and as far as she knew, his opening day was tomorrow. She didn't assume that his office would have a mass influx of patients on day one, but it would be interesting to have a business being run at the same time they were working with the kids.

"What time are they supposed to be here?" Celeste asked.

"Anytime now. Cassandra said the bus driver would bring three girls today."

"Do we know anything about them?"

"Not much. I just know there are two girls who are sixteen and one who is seventeen."

"I think I see them," Celeste said, pointing off in the distance as they stood on the front porch. Maybe they looked too eager, but they couldn't help it. Celeste would never admit it, but Abigail could tell that she was excited about the opportunity of working with the kids.

A small bus, actually more like an over-sized van, drove up in front of the house in the circular driveway. Cassandra got out, smiling and waving as the other doors opened.

Out popped three teenage girls, all looking very different from each other. The first one had blonde hair and looked like she belonged in a punk rock band. Her hair was bleached and spiky, she wore a tight red T-shirt with some band name Abigail didn't recognize, faded black skinny jeans and a pair of boots with spikes sticking out of them.

The next girl looked like she belonged in science club with her big, thick glasses, board straight brown hair and nondescript outfit.

Finally, there was a girl with jet black hair that was long enough to almost touch her rear end. She looked like a supermodel with her petite body, skinny jeans and skin tight pink sweater.

They started walking up the front steps, Cassandra still smiling as if she was forcing it. Being cooped up in a van with three teenage girls probably wasn't her favorite thing to do.

"Welcome, everyone!" Abigail said, matching Cassandra's smile. The girls all grunted, barely making eye contact.

"Girls, this is Abigail and Celeste," she said, pointing at each of them. Celeste nodded her head, only slightly cracking a smile. She would definitely never work in the hospitality industry.

"We are so glad to have you ladies here, and we can't wait to work with you over the next few weeks."

Again, Abigail wasn't getting much out of them.

"This is Tabatha," Cassandra said, pointing at the girl, who could only be described as looking a little nerdy.

"So nice to meet you, Tabatha."

"And this is Veronica," Cassandra said, pointing at the supermodel girl. "And, finally, this is Galaxy."

Abigail almost swallowed her tongue. Galaxy? Someone named their child Galaxy?

"Great to have you girls here. Why don't we go ahead inside and get to know each other a bit?" Abigail said. Cassandra quickly said her goodbyes and made her way back to the van, speeding off before they could even get into the sitting room.

As Abigail shut the door behind them, she pointed for everyone to go into the sitting room. She had no idea what she was going to say to these girls, and a part of her hoped Celeste would step up and take the wheel.

"Okay, listen, before we get started with anything, I want you to know that I aged out of this very same foster care system. And now I'm a successful businessperson, so I will not be taking any of your lame excuses about why you can't do something," Celeste said before sitting down and crossing her arms. Now Abigail really wished that she hadn't allowed Celeste to start the conversation.

"If you're such a prominent business person, then why are you wasting your time teaching us stuff?" Galaxy crossed her arms and leaned back in her chair, matching Celeste's stance. It was obvious this girl would not be easy.

"That's actually a good question, but it's

also none of your business. You're here to learn, so open your ears and shut your mouth."

Abigail wanted to run out of the room. She couldn't believe how Celeste was acting toward these girls that she had only just met, but it reminded her of living with Celeste for those two years. She had always been on the defensive like this.

"Celeste, can I talk to you in the foyer for a moment?" she said, forcing herself to smile.

Celeste said nothing, but stood up and walked out into the foyer, her arms crossed yet again.

"What do you want?"

"Don't you think you're coming on a bit harsh? You know nothing about these girls yet."

She laughed under her breath. "Oh, I know a lot about these girls. Especially that Galaxy kid. Who names their kid Galaxy?"

"Right?" Abigail agreed with her on that, but she didn't agree with Celeste's approach.

"You can't judge a book by its cover. And maybe they need a softer touch."

"Look, if you expect me to pussyfoot around these girls, I will not do it. If you don't toughen them up, they will get walked over in this world."

Abigail knew she had a point about that, but she certainly didn't agree with her methods. "Maybe we can find a happy medium."

"Fine, I'll try to be nicer, but I still stand by what I said. If we're not real with them, we're not going to make a difference in their lives."

Abigail chose not to argue anymore and turned to walk back into the sitting room. Celeste walked past her and leaned against the windowsill, first crossing her arms and then dropping them when Abigail made eye contact with her.

"We want to welcome you all here. We're going to be spending several weeks together getting you ready for the day when you are adults and out living life on your own."

"You mean you want to prepare us because none of us are getting adopted and we're basically going to be thrown out into the world on our butts," Veronica said. Her voice, sounding much like an eighties valley girl, made Abigail's ears hurt.

"I didn't say that…"

"You didn't have to. We already know what's up. We know we're not getting adopted, and we know you're only doing this because you feel bad for us." Tabatha, the quiet one, fidgeted with her hands as she stared down at her lap. Abigail knew what that felt like to be so incredibly shy that you just wanted to sink backwards into the chair until you disappeared.

"Listen, you're right. You're not getting adopted. Nobody adopts a sixteen or seventeen-year-old kid. You're not cute, and you're probably a bunch of troublemakers," Celeste said, obviously giving up on the tactic of being nice.

"Celeste!"

"I'm not a troublemaker. I'm a good kid,"

Tabatha said, tearing up. "But nobody wants the nerdy kid."

"I think we're getting off on the wrong foot," Abigail said.

Celeste stood up. "I know how all of you feel. I was abandoned at the fire station when I was three years old by my own mother. She knew me, but she didn't love me enough to keep me. And then I went from foster home to foster home and then to a group home before the system threw me out on my butt. And it was hard. Nobody told me anything. But I'm standing here now, and I have a decent life. The point of this place is to give you the skills so that when you do get thrown out on your butt, you can stand up, dust yourself off and go for your dreams."

Abigail couldn't believe what she was hearing. Her eyes were literally welling with tears as she listened to the strange motivational speech that Celeste had just given.

"Your mom left you at the fire station?" Veronica said, her annoying voice going up a couple of octaves.

"She did."

"Wow, what a witch," she said, scrunching up her nose. "My mom was a heroin addict. She died," she said it with such a matter-of-fact tone that Abigail had to wonder if she had even dealt with the grief of something like that.

"Sorry to hear that, Veronica. I'm sure that was hard," Abigail said.

"Not really. She was awful. We lived in a trailer park. At least in foster care, I've gotten to live in actual houses. And when I turn eighteen, I'm going to get my own apartment and a new car."

Celeste let out a big laugh. "And how do you think you're going to do that?"

"I'm going to be a model, so I'll be making a lot of money."

"How do you become a model, exactly?"

"You just have to get discovered."

"And how do you get discovered?"

"I don't know! Why are you being so nosy?" she said, twirling her hair around one of her fingers.

"She's not being nosy, you idiot. She's trying to point out that you're not pretty enough to be a model," Galaxy said. Abigail put her hand on her forehead. How in the world were they going to get through to these three girls?

* * *

CELESTE WAS EXHAUSTED. Spending the first day with those three girls had wiped her out in ways she couldn't describe. Abigail had already gone to take a hot bath and lay down, but she was still too keyed up to take a nap.

Spending time with them reminded her of being in the system. All the emotions of that time in her life had been rushing back to her all day. The feelings of abandonment. The frustration of trying to fit in. The worry over how to be an adult. Celeste could remember how crushing all of it had been to her younger self.

She poured the bag of pasta into the pot

of boiling water, added a little salt and stirred it before leaning against the counter, closing her eyes to rest them. A simple meal of marinara sauce over noodles was going to have to suffice for dinner, as she couldn't bring herself to do anything more involved. How in the world did teachers handle being trapped with a bunch of ornery kids all day? She had a new respect for them.

"Cooking up some dinner?"

Startled, Celeste opened her eyes to see Ben standing there. "You scared me to death! What're you still doing here?" She wasn't used to somebody else being in the house all day.

"Sorry," he said, laughing. "I had some insurance paperwork to fill out. Figured I'd do it in my new office."

"Tomorrow is opening day, huh?"

"Yep. I have three patients scheduled."

"Wow, big first day."

"So, what are you cooking?"

Celeste sighed. "A bag of pasta and a jar of marinara."

He scrunched his nose like he smelled something terrible. "That sounds boring."

"Well, I didn't ask you to eat it," she said, laughing as she sat down on one of the stools at the breakfast bar.

"How did your first day with the girls go?"

"Awful. Our accountant got delayed and couldn't make it today, so we had to teach about household budgets. Talk about watching their eyes glaze over. Boring, boring stuff."

"Do you really want to eat that pasta?"

She looked over at the stove. "Not even a little bit."

"How about we make a deal?"

She rested her chin on her hand. "What kind of deal?"

"You let me buy you pizza at Valentino's, and afterward we can come back here and you can help me design a front desk area?"

"A front desk area?"

"Yeah. I need a nice area to welcome patients, and the desk I have for that is way too small. I thought maybe you could help me?"

Celeste built houses for a living, or at least she used to, but she could also build just about anything that required wood. "Doesn't Dawson build furniture?"

"He does, but he's so busy right now, and I thought since you're right here…"

Celeste started laughing. "Fine, I'll help you, but only because I'm starving and I love a good pizza. Let me turn off this pasta and grab my keys."

ABIGAIL'S EYES fluttered open when she heard the front door shut. She stood up slowly, stretching her arms high above her head as she peeked out the window to see what was going on.

She saw Celeste and Ben walking down the sidewalk, chatting as they moved along. At least it seemed like Celeste was able to make one friend in town, even if it wasn't her.

She rubbed the sleep from her eyes and headed downstairs to find something for dinner, since it seemed her roommate did that without her. It wasn't like she expected Celeste to cook her dinner every night, but they'd had a long day, and she assumed they would sit together at the table and at least have a conversation about how it went.

She made her way into the kitchen, where she saw a pot of pasta that had not been cooked. Sticking her finger in the water and noticing it it was still pretty warm, she turned it back on. There was also a jar of marinara sauce sitting on the counter. She wasn't sure why Celeste had chosen not to cook it, but she wasn't too proud to eat it herself.

After a few minutes, she was able to make herself a bowl of pasta, and she located a couple of garlic bread sticks that were still in the freezer. After heating them in the microwave, she put everything onto a tray and carried it back upstairs. No need to sit at the kitchen table alone when she could sit in her bed.

As she passed Celeste's room, she noticed the door was open and some of Elaine's journals were sitting on the bed. She had wondered where they went. The first day they were going through things, they had found them in a box, but then Abigail had never seen them again.

She went to her room, put down her tray, and walked across the hall to Celeste's room. She figured she would look through some of the journals since Celeste had never told her she did or what they said. Then she would quickly toss them back onto her bed before she knew they were missing.

She sat down on the bed, holding two of the journals, and leaned back against the fluffy pillows. At first, she had wanted to stay in Elaine's room, but she actually enjoyed the guest room. It had a beautiful view overlooking the square and part of the ocean.

Plus, she liked the bigger shower and the plush bed.

After taking a few bites of pasta, she opened the first journal and started reading. A lot of it was Elaine talking about being a foster mother and her frustrations.

Then there were entries about some of the smaller kids that had been staying there at the same time as Abigail and Celeste. There were entries about Abigail and how sweet she was, what an excellent student and how kind she was to other people.

And then there were other passages about Celeste and how difficult she was. How hard it was to be her foster mother. How much she was getting into trouble at school. None of that was a surprise to Abigail, having lived through it.

But then she came to passages where it was obvious that Elaine had loved Celeste. And when she saw Elaine had even considered adopting her at one point, Abigail was shocked. There was no mention of her ever wanting to adopt Abigail, and that broke her heart.

All these years, she had silently agreed with Celeste that Elaine liked her better. She wondered why Elaine had never attempted to adopt her, and now here she read that not only did she not want to adopt Abigail, but she had thought of adopting Celeste instead.

She slammed the journal closed and stared straight ahead, her pasta getting colder and colder. How could this be true? How could Elaine have wanted to be Celeste's mother and not hers? They'd had such a wonderful relationship while she lived there, and an even better one in the decades following. Never once had Elaine mentioned that she had wanted to adopt Celeste.

How had she been wrong about this woman she loved so much? Here she was trying to do such good things in the name of a woman who didn't even want her?

In that moment, none of it made sense to her. She almost wanted to pack her bags and leave, but she realized that was ridiculous.

She was a grown woman now who had built a life for herself, and walking away from making that much money on a house was not something she was prepared to do.

She laid her head back and closed her eyes, hoping to fall asleep again. Suddenly, she didn't have an appetite for dinner.

CHAPTER 11

"$\mathcal{A}$re you sure we're going to have enough room up here? I would hate for the pastor to fall off the top of this lighthouse!" Julie said, laughing. She and Janine had gone to the top of the lighthouse to lay out the floor plan for the wedding.

Janine had finally decided to do the service at the top but have a big party at Julie's afterward. That way, nobody felt excluded by not being at the actual wedding.

Even though Emma had helped them clear out space in the gallery, and the doors would open, there was still going to be very little room.

"I think we'll be fine. We can fit Meg and Christian here, Colleen and Tucker over here," she said, moving from side to side inside the gallery. "You'll be standing up next to me, and Dawson will stand next to William…"

"And where will Dixie be?"

"She will sit right here, like the mother of the bride," she said, smiling.

"What about your *own* mother?"

Janine stopped in her tracks, putting her hand over her mouth as her eyes widened. "How did I forget our mother?"

"I don't know, but let's not share that little tidbit with her. And where are we supposed to put Harry? And Nick? And little Vivi?"

Janine sighed. "Why does everything have to be so hard?"

Julie felt bad. Her sister was already under so much stress about the wedding, and she was only adding to it by asking so many questions. "Look, Meg can hold a baby in her lap, so that's no big deal. Mom and Dixie can just sit very close together. And I'm sure that Harry and Nick wouldn't mind just meeting us at the party."

"Do you think so? I don't want to offend them…"

"Janine, this is your wedding. You want to have it at the top of the lighthouse, and that's exactly what we're going to do. We will fit who we need to fit, and everybody else can just deal with it."

"Do you think I'm being difficult wanting to get married up here?"

Julie put her hands on Janine's shoulders. "No, I don't. I think it's lovely, and we will make it happen. You just focus on breathing and getting ready to be William's wife, okay?"

Julie and Janine finished up and walked back down the stairs. When they reached the bottom, Julie was shocked to see her two daughters and her granddaughter standing there.

"Oh, my gosh! When did you get home?"

Julie said, running and immediately scooping Vivi up before hugging both of her daughters.

"Well, you didn't think we were going to miss the wedding, did you?" Meg said, laughing as she hugged her aunt Janine.

"I knew you'd get home in time, but the wedding isn't for a few more weeks. I'm just so happy to have you both here. And look at my granddaughter! You're practically big enough to go to high school now," she said, hugging her tightly. Vivi laughed and then wiggled down onto the ground where she could run around.

"Congratulations on your engagement!" Janine said to Colleen as she gave her a big hug.

"Thank you. I can't believe I'm going to join the old married women's club soon," she said, laughing.

"Well, it's a wonderful club to be a part of," Julie said, patting the top of Vivi's head as she twirled beside her. She couldn't believe how much bigger she was just in the last few weeks.

"Is there anything we can do to help with the wedding?" Meg asked.

"Oh, you might regret asking that question," Janine said, putting her arm around Meg as they walked toward the road.

* * *

As the days passed, it got easier and easier to teach the girls about life skills. Tabatha started opening up and being less shy. She was actually a pretty cool kid, if Celeste wanted to admit that out loud.

Then there was Veronica, whose name suited her well. She was what Celeste would have described as a snob in school, and she could easily see why no one had adopted her. She was a different kind of "prickly" than Celeste, but it still didn't make her overly endearing to potential adoptive parents.

But Celeste was most interested in Galaxy. She was tough, determined, and outspoken. Of course, that reminded Celeste a lot of herself. She could also see the flaws in Galaxy, and she hoped to help her navigate those personality traits that might make assimilating into adult life more difficult for her.

"So, are you working on your résumé?" She sat down next to Galaxy at the picnic table in the backyard overlooking the ocean. Rhonda, the human resources director they had roped into teaching the girls about making a résumé, had given them an assignment. They had to write an objective which would help potential employers know what they were looking for in a job. Then they had to write about all the skills they had for the job.

Galaxy sat there, staring down at the notebook and pencil in front of her. "I don't see what the point of this is."

"The point is so that you know how to market yourself to get a job when you turn eighteen and are out on your own."

"It isn't hard to get a job. I see signs

asking for help wanted everywhere," she said, rolling her eyes.

"Yeah, but do you want to work a job where you're making eight dollars an hour slinging hamburgers, or do you want to work a job where you're making fifteen dollars an hour working in a nice air-conditioned office?"

"It doesn't really matter. I'm going to buy an old vintage van, fix it up and travel all over the country. I'm going to play my guitar on street corners and make money that way."

Celeste held her tongue to the point that she almost bit it in half. Had she been this full of herself at that age? Probably.

"And how are you going to buy the van?"

"I don't know. They can't be that expensive."

Celeste laughed. "A vintage van? You're looking at several hundred dollars if you get something that doesn't even have a motor. Do you know how to repair vehicles?"

"Well, no."

"So you'll have to pay a mechanic, and they are even more expensive."

Galaxy looked at her. "Did you go to college?"

"No, I didn't."

"My foster mom is trying to force me to apply for colleges. I don't want to go to college."

"Then don't. You don't have to have an expensive education to be a successful person."

"I just don't see why I can't do what I want to do."

"Listen, I felt the same way when I was your age. But here's the thing. You have to *earn* the right to do what you want. You weren't born with a silver spoon in your mouth, right?"

"A silver spoon? What the heck does that mean?"

"Nevermind. What I'm saying is you weren't born into wealth. Neither was I. And that just meant that I had to work harder than everybody else."

"That's what I'm planning to do. Play my guitar and make money."

"What are you going to do when businesses kick you off the sidewalk? Or some other musician gets more attention? What are you going to do when it rains or snows? Or when your van breaks down and you don't have heat?"

"So you're saying I have to go to college?"

"No. But you need an education and a stable job if you want to live a decent life outside of foster care. Once you make enough money, you can tell everybody to kiss your hindquarters and then do what you want. But for now, you need to make a plan that's better than buying an imaginary van."

Galaxy sighed and picked up the pencil. "Fine. Explain what this objective thing is again."

"Do you think we're getting through to them at all?" Abigail asked as they sat at the kitchen table, eating sandwiches for dinner.

"I don't know. It's up to them whether or not they want to take our advice. I think I got through to Galaxy a little bit today, or maybe she was just humoring me," Celeste said, biting on a particularly crisp dill pickle.

"Can I ask you something?"

"Can I stop you?"

"Did you read any of Elaine's journals?"

Celeste froze in place, holding her sandwich in mid-air while she stared down at the table. It was a brief pause, but plenty for Abigail to know that she read the same thing she did.

"Why?"

"Because I think you read them, and then I read them."

Celeste dropped her sandwich and stared at Abigail. "So you're telling me you went into my room and took the journals off my bed?"

Abigail bit her lip. "I saw them when I passed by..."

"Seriously? I can't even get some privacy in my own room?"

"Look, I'm sorry. It was probably the wrong thing to do…"

"Probably?"

"I said I'm sorry. But what I'm getting at is that I was surprised by what I read."

"You mean you were surprised that Elaine wanted to adopt me and not you?"

Abigail took a deep breath, pushing it forcefully out her nose until her nostrils flared out like she was a bull about to attack.

"I just don't understand. We had a wonderful relationship for so many years, and she would have chosen you to adopt? You've said a million times she didn't like you!"

Celeste shook her head. "So, let me get this straight. You're upset because the woman who left us this million dollar house wanted to adopt me, but didn't, several decades ago?"

"I'm not mad, just hurt."

Celeste rolled her eyes and stood up, her hands on her hips. "Well, shall we all dab our eyes with tissues over the sorrow we feel for Abigail not getting something she wanted?"

"You don't have to be rude about it," Abigail said through gritted teeth.

"Come on! This is just typical of you. Everything must go perfectly for little miss perfect Abigail. And things should always go horribly wrong for horrible Celeste, right?"

Abigail stood up. "You know that's not what I meant!"

"Then what did you mean, Abby?"

"Abigail." She'd never felt the urge to strangle someone, but her hands were starting to spasm under the pressure.

"Even your name has to be perfect!"

"Look, I wasn't saying you didn't deserve to be adopted, but she said she loved me. She was so motherly to me. Why didn't she want me?" Without warning, tears spilled over and fell down her cheeks.

Celeste ran her fingers through her hair. "I was just as surprised as you were when I read that in her journal. I've spent my whole life thinking that Elaine Benson hated me, so

I wasn't expecting to read that. I was honestly expecting her to write sonnets about you."

Abigail giggled. "So was I!"

Surprisingly, Celeste laughed at that. Slowly, they both sat down, each of them still laughing. "I guess we didn't know a lot about the old woman like we thought we did."

"I guess not. Apparently, she hated me."

Celeste rolled her eyes. "Abigail, she didn't hate you. You just didn't need her as much as I did."

Abigail was surprised to hear her admit she needed someone back in those days. "You needed her?"

"I didn't think so at the time, but I needed somebody. I needed a mother. Who doesn't? Heck, I still need a mother."

"When I got adopted, I was so devastated and depressed. I wanted to be Elaine's daughter. I love my adoptive parents, but they never really got me like she did. They never understood me. I felt very different for the rest of my adolescence."

"Well, now you know how I've felt my entire life. I still feel that way. I don't fit in anywhere."

"You seem to fit in with Ben Callaway," she said, smiling slyly.

"What is that supposed to mean?" Celeste asked, leaning back in her chair and crossing her arms.

"I'm just saying that the two of you seem to be hitting it off."

"I think you're over exaggerating, as you commonly do. At most, he's an acquaintance."

"Do you go out and eat dinner with acquaintances often?"

"I don't go out and eat dinner with anyone often. This is very new to me. People in this town want to socialize, and I'd rather just be left alone."

"You can say that if you want, Celeste, but I don't believe that. I think you're interested in Ben."

Celeste stood up and walked over to the refrigerator, grabbing another bottle of water before turning around. "Look, I'm not the kind of woman that men really want to date. I'm tall, mouthy, super independent. I learned a long time ago not to expect any kind of white picket fence in my future."

Abigail walked across the kitchen and leaned against the counter. "You should be open to that."

"Why? So that I can have yet another person in my life disappoint me at some point? No thanks."

"Just as an outsider, I'm saying that I think Ben is interested in you. And he's a nice guy. A doctor."

"I'm not impressed with money or titles. Besides, if you and I can keep from killing each other, we'll both have half a million dollars in a couple of months."

"Money won't keep you warm at night," Abigail said, as she walked out of the kitchen.

"If you get a big enough stack of it, it surely will!" Celeste called back. Abigail giggled as she walked up the stairs to her room.

* * *

"WHY DID you pick such an intricate plan?" Ben complained as he continued helping Dawson build what had to be the largest table in human history.

"I didn't pick it. This is a custom order. Remember the Remington family over off of Oak Grove Drive?"

"You mean the mansion on the water? The old man who invented some super special plumbing device that made him a gazillionaire?"

"That's the one. Well, his granddaughter owns the place now and has seven kids. She wanted me to create a special kitchen table that could be passed down for the next few generations. And then she went on Google and found this picture which I had to customize to fit her brood of kids."

"The cost of the wood alone has to be astronomical."

"Trust me, it was. But, we're almost finished and then we just have to do the final

glaze because she wants it to be extra
shiny."

"Rich people are weird."

Dawson laughed. "Says the doctor."

"Listen, I'm not the kind of doctor that
makes a million dollars a year. I'm much
more interested in making my patient well.
That means I don't get as much repeat business as one might hope."

"How are you liking it over there? Is the
new office working out okay?"

"I've had a steady stream of patients. It's a
really nice space and should suit me well for a
while. At least until something else opens up."

"Can I ask you a question?"

"Of course."

"Are you interested in Celeste?"

Ben coughed and then cleared his throat.
"What would give you that idea?"

"I'm not blind, man. I saw how interested
you were talking to her at dinner, and then a
little birdie told me they saw you eating
pizza together the other night."

He laughed and shook his head. "The gossip mill in this town is faster than anything I've ever seen."

"You still haven't answered my question," Dawson said, rubbing sealant onto the top of the table.

"She's nice, and we've had a fun time chatting here and there. But I just got a divorce, and I'm in no hurry to get back into a relationship with anybody."

"Did I ever tell you about how Julie landed in Seagrove?"

"I don't think so."

"She had been married to a man for twenty-one years. He came home one day from a business trip and told her he had another woman in a different city and a new baby."

"Wow. That sounds like something out of a bad TV movie."

"Right? Anyway, they were supposed to buy a beach house together. It had been Julie's dream for years. Instead, they divorced, and she came to Seagrove alone after having bought a cottage sight unseen."

"Probably not the best thing to do."

"Probably not. Thankfully, there was this handsome, dashing contractor who was ultra talented, and he ended up helping her renovate the place."

"And quite a humble guy, it seems."

"And it wasn't immediate, but we became friends and then we became more than friends. She was the same as you, not wanting to get into anything too serious after coming out of a long marriage. But the way I see it, if the right person comes along, it doesn't really matter what happened in your past."

"I get what you're saying, but I can't go through it again. Divorce is the hardest thing I've ever had to do."

"I know, but I also know that if you find the woman for you, you can't delay. You have to take *courageous action*."

"Courageous action? Have you been reading self-help books?"

"Maybe. But it's true. Putting yourself out there after such a terrible time in your life takes courage. And finding the woman of your dreams, your true soulmate, takes action."

"I'll keep it in mind. For now, can we finish this table and get out of this hot barn so I can drink about a gallon of sweet tea?"

Dawson laughed. "Fine. You're such a baby."

CHAPTER 12

*A*fter their talk in the kitchen a week ago, Celeste and Abigail had gotten along much better. It seemed like they were more on the same page, which wasn't something Celeste had ever anticipated happening. She found Abigail less annoying, which was like a miracle straight from God.

"Okay, girls, today we're going to talk about renting your first apartment."

"Why can't it be a house?" Galaxy blurted out.

"It could be a house, but the chances of you getting approved and having enough money to rent a house are slim to none," Celeste said matter-of-factly.

"Most apartments will require you to get a credit check. At your age, you may not have a credit score yet, and they will often ask for a person to cosign," Abigail said as they stood in front of the girls. They were sitting in the kitchen at the table, notebooks in front of them.

"Most people would get their parents to cosign, but that's not possible for you ladies, so we have to think outside of the box," Celeste said.

"So what are we supposed to do?" Veronica asked.

"There are a couple of options. You can start building your credit when you turn eighteen by getting a secured credit card. Save up some money, send it to the credit card company and they will give you a secured card. You must make payments on time every single month and never charge the card all the way up to the limit. That will help you build a credit score, but it's going to take you some time."

"But we don't have time," Galaxy shouted out again.

"There are some landlords that may give you a break, being that you're going to be eighteen years old, but you have to be a responsible adult. For example, you need to be able to show them you've had a steady job and that you get paid every week or two weeks. You have to prove to them that you are a good risk," Celeste said.

"Why does everything have to be so hard?" Tabatha suddenly said.

"Excuse me?" Abigail responded.

"Like, we got left by our families. We had no control over that. And now, the very people who are supposed to be taking care of us are going to kick us out into the world with no parachute. It's not fair. We make mistakes because no one ever taught us!" Tabatha said, throwing her hands in the air. Celeste had never seen her get ruffled, and she certainly hadn't seen her show any kind of anger.

"I understand how hard this is. Trust me, I do. I remember the first day that I was officially out of the foster care system. I was standing outside of the social services building with my backpack. Everything I owned was in that backpack, and it wasn't much. Thankfully, I had worked a part-time job for a few months, so I had about two hundred dollars to my name. I ended up sleeping behind a building for the first several weeks, dodging people so that nobody would turn me into the police."

The girls sat there in stunned silence, staring at Celeste. "So you were like homeless?" Veronica asked.

"I was. Then, I met this girl who agreed to let me sleep on her sofa until I could get on my feet. I paid the electric bill instead of rent, but then she got evicted, so I got kicked out. Thankfully, I had accumulated enough cash at my two jobs to rent a really crappy one-bedroom apartment in a seedy part of town. Every night, I would hear gunshots. Not the best lullaby."

"So how did you get out of that?" Galaxy asked. Celeste noticed that Abigail had stopped talking and was just standing against the wall like she was in shock.

"Work. Plain old hard work. But, you see, what you can learn from this is that if you prepare yourself before you leave the system, you can have what you need to get started. Don't be like me and put on your blinders and think that you're a superhero and nothing's going to touch you. Be smart. Plan ahead. Build your credit now, work some jobs, save some money. Stop spending money on stupid crap like make up and fast food."

"I have to go," Tabatha suddenly said, running out of the room and down the hallway into the bathroom. Celeste looked at Abigail, who shrugged her shoulders.

"Does anybody know what's wrong with her?" Celeste asked. The girls just sat there, staring straight ahead like deer in the headlights."I'll take that as a yes. Somebody needs to fess up and tell us what's going on so we can help her."

"We can't break the pact," Veronica said.

"What pact?" Abigail asked.

"You know how it is. We are the closest things to sisters we have, even though we can't stand each other for the most part. But when somebody tells you a secret, you keep it," Galaxy said.

"Fine. Abigail, continue talking to them about apartments and credit while I go find Tabatha."

As Celeste walked out of the room, she was surprised to see Ben standing there in the hallway. He looked startled.

"Were you listening to our conversation?"

"I'm sorry. I was coming out of my office, and I couldn't help but overhear. The acoustics are crazy in this place."

"That's called eavesdropping," she said, irritated.

"I was coming to see if you wanted to have lunch today."

"Look, I appreciate the invite, but I've got a lot of things going on right now. I really don't have time for whatever this is that's happening." She pointed her hand back and forth between them.

"What?"

"I don't know if you're interested in me or what, but I have to tend to these girls. I can't let them go out on the street and be like I was. So, thanks, but no thanks," she said, turning quickly and heading down the hall toward the bathroom.

CELESTE STOOD outside of the bathroom door. "Tabatha, come out and talk to me."

"I can't," she said through sobs. It had been ten minutes, and Celeste had made no progress getting her out of there.

"Can I help?" Ben asked, quietly.

"I told you I can't do this right now," Celeste said, pursing her lips.

"I don't know what you think is going on,

but I'm not trying to do anything. I'm asking if you need my help as a professional who works with children."

She sighed. "Sorry. I guess I misunderstood. And yes, if you think you can get this kid out of the bathroom, please do." She stepped back and crossed her arms.

"What's her name?"

"Tabatha. She just freaked out and ran out of the meeting. We don't even know what's wrong and the other girls won't tell us."

He tapped on the door. "Hi, Tabatha. This is Dr. Callaway. I heard you're having a hard time right now, and I'd love to see if I can help you."

There was total silence. "I don't think you're going to be able to help her," Celeste said.

"Tabatha, there's nothing you're dealing with that I haven't dealt with before. I promise."

A few more moments of silence. Then, the door cracked open, and Tabatha's tear-stained face protruded from it slightly. "It's really bad."

"Would you like to come to my office right there down the hall? We can talk about it and figure out what we need to do so that you can stop crying and feel better."

"Okay," she said, slowly opening the door and following him to his office. He opened the door and let her in. Celeste followed closely behind, but Ben turned around and stopped her.

"I'm sorry, but you can't come in without her consent."

"These are *my* girls," she said, getting irritated.

"No, these are not *your* girls, Celeste. You're not their parent. Now, if you'll excuse us." He closed the door behind them, and Celeste never felt more helpless in her life.

* * *

"What do you think is going on?" Abigail asked as she and Celeste sat nervously at the kitchen table. Veronica and Galaxy had gone out to the beach for a little break, but that was mainly because Abigail sent them there.

"I don't know, but it's big, whatever it is."

As if on cue, the door opened to Ben's office, and he walked into the kitchen, his arm around the top of Tabatha's shoulder. Her face was red and puffy from crying, but at least she had stopped sobbing.

"Are you okay, Tabatha?" Abigail asked.

"Not really," she said, softly.

"Tabatha would like to share something with the both of you, and I would ask that you listen to her and be supportive."

Celeste and Abigail nodded as Tabatha slowly sat down across from them."I don't think I can say it. Dr. Callaway, can you tell them?"

"Sure, Tabatha," he said, patting her on the shoulder. "Tabatha is pregnant."

"Oh my gosh," Celeste said without thinking.

"What can we do?" Abigail said.

"Obviously, we have to alert her social

worker, who will tell her foster parents. And I think there may be some law-enforcement that needs to get involved in this particular situation."

"Law-enforcement?" Tabatha said, starting to cry again.

"Tabatha was violated by an older boy who is also staying in her foster home."

"No. You can't call the cops. They'll kick me out!"

"Honey, you can't continue to live there with the person who hurt you. That's not right. Let us help you." Abigail said.

"She can live here," Celeste said, the words popping out of her mouth before she knew they were coming.

"What?" Ben said.

"Surely we can get some kind of emergency order where she can live here and be safe. Plus, you're right here and you can provide some medical care."

"Celeste, I'm a pediatrician, not an OB/GYN."

"Okay, fine, I'll find her another doctor

for that. But she can't go back there. Not even for one night. Call the social worker right now because this kid is not going back to that house. And those parents should be prosecuted for not paying better attention…"

"Celeste, calm down. You're not helping things getting irate," Abigail said, whispering in her ear.

"I'm sorry. Tabatha, this isn't your fault. You were taken advantage of at a very vulnerable time in your life, and I understand what that feels like. But we will get you through this."

"How far along is she?" Abigail asked.

"Obviously we can't be sure until she meets with an OB/GYN, but from the dates she told me I think she's about four months along."

"I'm sixteen years old. I can't raise a baby. I don't even have a job."

"Don't worry about any of that right now, Tabatha. You've got months before the baby would come," Abigail said.

"I can't have an... I can't even say the word."

"You don't have to do that either. Don't make any choices right now. Let's calm down and talk to your social worker first, okay?" Celeste said, reaching across the table and taking her hand.

LEARNING how to live with a teenager in the house all the time had been difficult, to say the least. Celeste wasn't used to acting like a mother, but what Tabatha needed right now was mothering.

She and Abigail had come together in a way that she would've never believed had she not seen it with her own eyes. They had helped Tabatha move in, been with her through the process of being interviewed by police and also helped her with life skills, homework and everything else that a teenage girl needed.

As they moved through the process, Celeste had to admit she had a greater respect for Elaine Benson. Of course, Celeste hadn't found herself pregnant, but she had been difficult. Actually, much more difficult than Tabatha. The kid was actually pretty easy going, a good student and even cleaned up after herself.

She had also been delighted to see how Galaxy and Veronica had come together to support Tabatha. In fact, it was miraculous in a way to see the transformation of the girls.

"I have a big announcement," Galaxy said, standing in front of their small group. They only had another few days together before the group was over and the girls would start moving on to the next part of their lives.

"I hope it's not like my announcement!" Tabatha said, joking. Although there were days she cried a lot, she was getting more used to being pregnant and the thought of what she would choose to do in the future. She still hadn't decided whether she would attempt to raise the child on her own or allow it to be adopted.

"No, nothing like that. But, I did get a job!"

Celeste, Abigail and the other two girls clapped their hands. "Really? That's amazing! What kind of job?" Abigail asked.

"I'm actually going to be working at a music studio near Charleston. They produce small to medium-sized artists, and I'm going to be the receptionist."

"Wow, Galaxy. I'm so impressed. And that will be the perfect job for you," Celeste said.

"Well, while we're doing announcements, I have something to say," Veronica said.

"Oh yeah? And what's that?" Abigail asked.

"So, like my foster parents are really pushy and they want me to go to college. So I started applying for scholarships and I actually got one! It's for this art school over in Savannah. I can't believe they accepted me, but as long as I work I should be able to afford it and live in university housing."

"Oh, my goodness! That's amazing, Veronica!" Abigail said.

"I have to say that we are so proud of you girls. All of you have come a long way in the last few weeks, and I know that you're prepared to go out into the world when it's time."

"We want to say thanks because we learned a lot," Galaxy said, handing them a card they had all signed.

"We've enjoyed it, a lot more than I thought we would," Celeste said, laughing.

She was trying to ignore the fact that later in the day, they would have their final judgment from Elaine's three friends. It felt so ridiculous to be nervous about it. They had done the best they could, even if they did end up with a pregnant teenager living with them temporarily.

They said goodbye to Veronica and Galaxy, although they would still come back for a few days. Tabatha went upstairs to take a nap, so Celeste and Abigail went into the kitchen to start dinner.

"Okay, you put in the dinner rolls, and I will check and see if the pot roast is done," Celeste said.

Abigail went over to the counter and picked up the package of rolls, pulling a cookie sheet out of the cabinet. "I'm really going to miss those young ladies. They finally grew on me after a while."

"Yeah, but I'm sure they will keep in touch. Social media, email, that sort of thing."

"I can't believe we did it. We actually made it through three months together," Abigail said, laughing.

"And somehow we ended up with a daughter," Celeste said, chuckling.

"So, I guess this is the end?"

Celeste turned off the slow cooker. "I don't know. I guess it depends on what the ladies say."

"And if they say we get the house, we sell?"

"I mean, is there really a reason to stay? We achieved our goal of doing something good."

"I suppose we did. But what about Tabatha?"

"I guess we would have to have social services place her somewhere else. She's definitely going to need support every day."

"I would really hate to uproot her. She's already been through so much turmoil."

Celeste walked over and sat down at the breakfast bar. "You know, I got a call from my old boss today. There's a new development twice the size of anything I've ever managed. He wants me to come back, but if we sell this place, I wouldn't have to do that kind of work anymore."

Abigail leaned against the counter. "I don't want to go back to public relations. I already know that.

"What do you want to do?"

"I don't know. I really enjoyed teaching these girls. I might want to continue doing something like that."

"I guess we shouldn't make any big decisions until we get judged. We may not even get this house, right?"

"Right. Well, I'd better get started on making the salad."

Celeste sat there for a moment, thinking about the options. They could sell the house and she could move on with her life like it never happened, with tons of money in her pocket. Or she could stay, continue to live in the house and find something to do in Seagrove.

Things with Ben had been strange since the day she spoke to him in the hallway before they found out Tabatha was pregnant. Maybe she had jumped to conclusions thinking he was interested in her. Either way, it was so embarrassing that she had tried to avoid him as best she could.

Of course, it was hard to do that when he was in her house most of the day working in his office. She would occasionally pass him in the hallway, but he hadn't made the mistake of asking her on a lunch date again. She had probably blown any chances she had with him.

Misreading other people's signals was her

gift. She had probably just imagined that he was interested in her, most likely because Abigail had suggested it.

Then, the other day, she saw him laughing and chatting with the mother of one of his patients out on the sidewalk. He handed her his card, and she smiled, sticking it into her pocket. Celeste assumed they were making a date or something. She couldn't blame him. The mother was probably well-adjusted and had been raised by actual human beings.

She decided not to decide until they had their meeting with Elaine's friends. There was nothing she could do until they decided if what she and Abigail had done was good enough to inherit a house.

ABIGAIL HAD NEVER BEEN MORE nervous in her life. She and Celeste were sitting in two chairs in the middle of an empty room. Dixie, SuAnn, and Henrietta had asked them to come over to the church fellowship hall. It was the most nondescript, empty room Abigail had ever seen.

There were two squeaky metal chairs in the middle of the room where Celeste and Abigail sat. Then there were three chairs, the same kind, directly in front of them, about ten feet away. She felt like they were about to get interrogated.

"Is this making you queasy, because it's making me queasy," Abigail said.

Celeste laughed. "No. But I am getting hungry. They must eat in here because it smells like meatloaf. Wait, maybe that's lasagna? What is that smell?"

"Would you hush about the smells? I'm a nervous wreck over here!"

"Sorry to keep you ladies waiting. Henrietta couldn't find her car keys," Dixie said, rolling her eyes and laughing. She walked over to Abigail and Celeste, shaking both of their hands before taking her seat. SuAnn waved from across the room, as did Henrietta, before both of them sat down. It was an awfully formal affair.

"As you know, you're here for your final judgment," Henrietta started. SuAnn chuckled under her breath.

"Oh, good Lord, you make it sound like they're standing at the gates of heaven waiting to find out if they got a ticket inside."

"We're supposed to be serious," Henrietta said, lightly smacking her on the leg.

"Ladies, you know why you're here. My two cohorts over here can't seem to get it together, so I'm going to take the reins," Dixie said, shooting both of them a glance that told them to be quiet.

"Thanks for meeting with us today," Abigail said. She immediately regretted it because it sounded like she was going to a job interview.

"We've had time to review everything that you've done with the house. We'd like to recap everything. For one, you allowed a pediatrician to move in, and that has been a blessing to the community. Second, you ran a program to help girls who are going to age out of the foster care system. And finally, it seems you've taken in one of those very same girls who has found herself with child."

"Yes, all of that is correct," Celeste said.

"We'd like to ask you some questions before we make our final decision. Celeste, what have you learned about yourself during this process?"

Abigail felt even more nervous. First, what were they going to ask her? She hadn't prepared for a speech or to answer essay questions. Second, what in the world was Celeste about to say? Anything could come out of her mouth at any moment.

"I learned I misjudged Elaine Benson all those years ago, and that she cared about me. I learned that dealing with a difficult teenager is very hard. And I learned I can let my guard down, somewhat, and be vulnerable with other people."

Abigail wanted to cry. The growth Celeste had shown by saying those things made her want to turn around in her chair and give her a huge hug, but she knew Celeste would probably just throw her across the room.

"Wonderful answer. Thank you. Abigail, what have you learned about yourself during this process?"

"I have learned that Celeste isn't as bad as I thought she was."

Suddenly, she couldn't think of anything else to say. The room was completely quiet as Celeste looked at her and the women shifted uncomfortably in their chairs. Then, without warning, all four of them burst out with laughter.

"Glad to hear it!" Celeste said, slapping her on the shoulder.

"Sorry. This kind of stuff makes me nervous. I learned a lot more about..."

Dixie waved her hand and laughed boisterously. "Don't worry, darlin', these questions are just a formality. We already agreed that you two ladies own the house!"

Celeste and Abigail smiled, stood up, and actually hugged each other. Abigail was afraid lightning was going to strike right there in the middle of the fellowship hall.

"We also have something else to share with you," Henrietta said.

Celeste and Abigail turned around and looked at them. "Okay, what's that?" Celeste said.

"Elaine directed that if we ended up giving you the house, we were also supposed to give you the entire contents of a specific bank account. Here is the latest statement from that account. She wanted you to know that there was another option besides selling the house and taking the money. If you wanted to continue living in Seagrove and doing good things with the house, this money will support you in that endeavor."

Henrietta handed the paper to them and they both looked at it, their mouths dropping open. A hefty six-figure sum. Abigail couldn't believe what she was seeing.

"So Elaine left us this money too?"

"She wanted you girls to have easier lives,

and she wanted you to stay here together if you chose to do so."

Abigail and Celeste stared at each other and then looked back down at the paper again. Neither of them had expected this. And neither of them had a clue what to do.

* * *

JANINE GRINNED as she and William drove up to Julie's house. The wedding had been the most perfect day of her life. Getting married at sunset with her closest family and friends had been everything she wanted it to be.

Now they were headed into the reception with tons of family and friends to surround them. Dawson and Julie had gone all out, hanging up string lights all over the deck area and opening the doors and windows of the home so that people could breeze in and out. There was food laid out everywhere and music playing.

People were already on the dance floor as

the DJ played music. Janine couldn't imagine a better ending to the best day of her life.

"Congratulations! We are so happy for you," Abigail said, giving Janine a hug.

"Thank you. We are ecstatic."

As they moved around the crowd, greeting everyone, Janine couldn't believe that she was finally William's wife. Everywhere they went, she held onto his hand for dear life.

"Are you two ready for your first dance?"

"Yes, we are!" William said to the DJ. They had already picked out a song, and when it started playing, William called Janine out onto the dance floor for their first dance as husband and wife.

As they swayed to the music, she thought back to all of their memories together all the way back to the first time they met. William had been so hard to read, so standoffish. And now, he was so kind, sweet and the perfect match for her.

She looked around the dance floor at friends and family laughing, talking, and dancing. She saw a little Vivi off in the distance, twirling around in her tulle dress.

It had taken her well into her forties to find the man of her dreams and get married, but it was already worth it and she'd only been married for half an hour.

* * *

"THIS IS A BEAUTIFUL RECEPTION," Celeste said to Julie as they stood off to the side of the dance floor, drinking a glass of wine.

"Thank you. It has been a magical day. I'm so happy for Janine and William."

"Me too. It's great to see two people so well-suited for each other."

"What about you? Are you seeing anyone special?"

Celeste laughed. "No. I'm just focused on helping Tabatha and figuring out my next move."

"Julie, I need you inside for a minute. The wedding cake..." Dawson said, looking panicked.

"Sorry, Celeste, I need to go see what's happening."

"No problem." Celeste watched her run off into the house. She took another sip of her wine and figured she would go tell Abigail that she was going to head home. She didn't really know many people at the reception, although she was very honored to be invited in the first place.

She put down her glass of wine and turned to look for Abigail.

"May I have this dance?" Ben was standing there, wearing a very stylish suit and holding out his hand.

"What?"

"At the risk of you thinking I'm going to propose marriage, I was just asking if maybe you might want to dance?"

"Look, I'm sorry about what I said that day. I was under a lot of stress…"

"I get it. I understand. But you still haven't answered me."

"I'm a terrible dancer. I will probably step on your feet."

"And I knocked you down because I was looking at a dog. We all have our faults."

Celeste laughed. "Okay, but if I break your toe, I'm not paying your medical bills."

They went out onto the dance floor, and he slipped his hands around her waist, forcing her to put her arms around his neck. It was much the way people danced in middle school.

"So, I hear you and Abigail got the house?"

"Yes, we did."

"At the risk of sounding like I'm worried about renting my office space, have you two decided what you're going to do?"

"Yeah. We actually have. We're going to stay, at least for now. We're not going to sell the place, so your office is safe."

Ben beamed. "I have to admit something."

"What's that?"

"I didn't really care about my office space."

"No?"

"No. I just didn't want you to leave Seagrove."

"Why not?"

"Celeste, you are one of the most difficult people I've ever met. You're spiky and have a tough outer shell, but I can't help it. I really like you. And I don't mean as a friend, and I hate that because I just got divorced, and I shouldn't be liking anybody. But dang it, I like you."

She couldn't help but laugh. "That's the strangest thing any man has ever said to me. But I think it's a compliment?"

"Yes, it's a compliment. And I know neither of us is ready for anything serious, but I'm glad you're staying. I'm glad you didn't run. And I hope one day you'll let me ask you out to lunch again."

She smiled. "I think that can be arranged."

DID you know Rachel Hanna has more than 30 books? Check out ALL of them on her website (along with links to each ebook store, large print, audio and more!) at www. RachelHannaAuthor.com

JOIN RACHEL'S amazing Facebook reader group at https://www.facebook.com/ groups/RachelReaders

CPSIA information can be obtained
at www.ICGtesting.com
Printed in the USA
LVHW090921091021
700001LV00007B/466

9 781953 334466